His lips met hers in a rush like the eagle falling on its prey.

Far from diving for cover, Dani's mouth rose to his and melded with it. Sensation crashed over her. She was dimly aware of their natural surroundings, the wind in the trees, animals scurrying nearby, and of his hands resting warmly at her waist, but her whole being focused on the kiss and the powerful and intense effect it created in her body. Heat flooded her core, spreading out to her limbs, squeezing the breath from her lungs as she gave herself over to the sensation.

She'd never experienced a kiss like this. Chemistry, was it? Or was it that she'd never kissed a man as gorgeous and dashing as Quasar? Either way the effect was overwhelming.

She had no idea how long they kissed, but when they finally pulled apart and she opened her eyes, she found herself blinking against now-unaccustomed daylight. "Oh, dear." The words spilled out.

Quasar gave an amused frown. "Oh, dear? That's not the effect I intended."

* * *

If you're on Twitter,
tell us what you think of Harlequin Desire!
#harlequindesire

Dear Reader,

Her Desert Knight is the third book in a series that was never intended to be a series. When I sold my first Harlequin Desire novel, *The Boss's Demand,* the story of Elan Al Mansur's romance with his assistant Sara was intended as a stand-alone. When the book came out, I received emails from readers asking if I planned to write stories for his two brothers, who were mentioned briefly in the final wedding scene.

It took me a few years to write *The Desert Prince,* about tradition-bound Salim's reunion with the unsuitable college girlfriend he tried to forget—and the child he never knew existed.

I had a hard time figuring out the story for Quasar, the youngest and wildest of the three brothers. What kind of woman would stop an international playboy in his tracks and make him rethink his freewheeling ways? Finally I had an idea and wrote *Her Desert Knight.* It's been more than seven years since the first book, so my apologies to those who have been patiently waiting all that time.

I hope you enjoy Quasar and Dani's story and please keep in touch!

Jen

HER DESERT KNIGHT

—

JENNIFER LEWIS

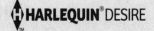

Recycling programs
for this product may
not exist in your area.

ISBN-13: 978-0-373-73353-8

Her Desert Knight

Printed in U.S.A.

Books by Jennifer Lewis

Harlequin Desire

^*The Prince's Pregnant Bride* #2082
^*At His Majesty's Convenience* #2094
^*Claiming His Royal Heir* #2105
Behind Boardroom Doors #2144
†*The Cinderella Act* #2170
†*The Deeper the Passion...* #2202
†*A Trap So Tender* #2220
Affairs of State #2234
A High Stakes Seduction #2334
Her Desert Knight #2340

Silhouette Desire

The Boss's Demand #1812
Seduced for the Inheritance #1830
Black Sheep Billionaire #1847
Prince of Midtown #1891
**Millionaire's Secret Seduction* #1925
**In the Argentine's Bed* #1931
**The Heir's Scandalous Affair* #1938
The Maverick's Virgin Mistress #1977
The Desert Prince #1993
Bachelor's Bought Bride #2012

**The Hardcastle Progeny*
^*Royal Rebels*
†*The Drummond Vow*

Other titles by this author available in ebook format.

JENNIFER LEWIS

has been dreaming up stories for as long as she can remember and is thrilled to be able to share them with readers. She has lived on both sides of the Atlantic and worked in media and the arts before she grew bold enough to put pen to paper. She would love to hear from readers at jen@jenlewis.com. Visit her website at www.jenlewis.com.

For my sister Annabel

Acknowledgments:

Many thanks to the readers who asked me for more stories about the Al Mansur brothers and fired my imagination to write them. Also thanks to my agent Andrea and the many people who read and improved those stories, especially my editors Demetria Lucas (book one), Diana Ventimiglia (book two), Charles Griemsman (book three).

One

Going to her favorite bookshop in Salalah was like stepping back into a chapter of *Arabian Nights*. To get there, Dani had to walk through the local souk, past the piles of carrots and cabbages, the crates of dates and figs, winding her way through knots of old men wearing their long dishdashas and turbans just as they must have done a thousand years ago.

Then there was the store itself. The double doorway of time-scarred wood was studded with big metal rivets, like the entrance to a castle. Only a small section opened, and she had to step over the bottom part of the door into the smoky darkness of the shop. The smoke was incense, eternally smoldering away in an antique brass burner that hung in one corner, mingled with pipe smoke from the elderly store owner's long, carved pipe. He sat in the corner, poring over the pages of a thick, leather-bound tome, as if he maintained the shop purely for his own reading pleasure. It was entirely possible that the store was a front of some kind, since there rarely seemed to be any customers, but that didn't diminish Dani's enjoyment of its calming atmosphere.

The books were piled on the floor like the oranges in the stalls outside. Fiction, poetry, treatises on maritime navigation, advice on the training of the camel: all were in Arabic and nearly all were at least fifty years old and bound in leather, darkened by the passage of many greasy fingers over their smooth, welcoming surfaces. She'd found several gems here, and always entered the shop with a prickle of anticipation, like someone setting out on a journey where anything could happen.

Today, as she stepped over the threshold and filled her lungs with the fragrant air, she noticed an unfamiliar visitor in the picturesque gloom of the interior. The light from one tiny, high window cast its diffuse glow over the tall, broad-shouldered figure of a young man.

Dani stiffened. She didn't like the idea of a man in her djinn-enchanted realm of magic books. She didn't like men anywhere at all, lately, but she gave the shop owner a pass as he was quiet and kind and gave her big discounts.

She resolved to slip past the stranger on her way to the stack she'd started to investigate yesterday: a new pile of well-thumbed poetry books the shop owner had purchased at a bazaar in Muscat. She'd almost bought one yesterday, and she'd resolved overnight that today she wasn't leaving without it.

The interloper was incongruously dressed in Western clothing—jeans and a white shirt, to be exact—with expensive-looking leather loafers on his feet. She eyed him suspiciously as she walked past, then regretted it when he glanced up. Dark blue eyes ringed by jet-black lashes peered right into hers. He surveyed her down the length of an aristocratic nose, and the hint of a smile tugged at his wide, arrogant-looking mouth. A younger, stupider Dani might have thought he was "cute," but she was not so foolish now. She braced herself in case he had the nerve to speak to her.

But he didn't. Slightly deflated, and kicking herself for thinking that anyone would want to speak to her at all, she headed for her familiar pile of books. Only to discover that the one she wanted was missing. She checked the stack twice. Then the piles on either side of it. In the dim, smoky atmosphere, it wasn't easy to read the faded spines, the gold-leaf embossing worn off by countless eager hands. Maybe she'd missed it.

Or maybe he was reading it.

She glanced over her shoulder, then jerked her head back when she discovered that the strange man was staring right at her. Alarm shot through her. Had he been watching her the whole time? Or had he just turned around at the exact same moment she had? She was annoyed to find her heart pounding beneath the navy fabric of her traditional garb.

"Are you looking for this book?" His low, velvety male voice made her jump, and she cursed herself for being so on edge.

He held out the book she'd been searching for. A 1930s edition of *Majnun Layla* by Persian poet Nizami Ganjavi, with a faded green leather binding and elaborate gold tooling.

"You speak English." The first words out of her mouth took her by surprise. She'd intended to say yes, but her brain short-circuited. She hadn't heard anyone speak English since she'd come back here from New Jersey three months ago. She'd begun to wonder if she'd ever use her hard-won language skills again.

He frowned and smiled at the same time. "Yes. I didn't even realize I was speaking English. I guess I've spent too much time in the States lately. Or maybe my gut instinct told me you speak it, too."

"I lived in the U.S. for a few years myself." She felt flustered. His movie-star looks were disconcerting, but she tried not to judge a book by its cover. She cleared her throat. "And yes, I mean, that is the book I was looking for."

"What a shame. I was about to buy it." He still spoke in English. His features and coloring looked Omani, but his Western clothing and ocean-colored gaze gave him a hint of exoticism. "You were here first." She shrugged, and tried to look as if she didn't care.

"I think not. If you knew it was here and were looking for it, clearly you were here first." Amusement danced in his unusual blue eyes. "Have you read it?"

"Oh, yes. It's a classic. I've read it several times."

"What's it about?"

"It's a tragic love story." How could he not know that? Maybe he didn't even read Arabic. He had a strange accent. British, maybe.

"Sometimes I think all love stories are tragic. Does anyone really live happily ever after?"

"I don't know. My own experience hasn't been very encouraging." As soon as she spoke she was shocked at herself. She'd resolved to keep her private torments secret.

"Mine, either." He smiled slightly. "Maybe that's why we like to read a tragic love story where everyone dies in the end, so our own disastrous efforts seem less awful by comparison." The light in his eyes was kind, not mocking. "Did you come back here to get away from someone?"

"I did." She swallowed. "My husband—ex-husband. I hope I never see him again." She probably shouldn't reveal so much to a total stranger. Divorce was rare and rather scandalous in Oman.

"Me, too." His warm smile relaxed her. "I live in the States myself but I come to Oman whenever I need to step off the carousel and feel some firm ground beneath my feet. It's always reassuring how little has changed here while I've been gone."

"I found that alarming when I first came back. If it wasn't for the cars and cell phones we could still be in the Dark Ages. My dad and brothers don't like me leaving the house without a male relative to escort me. What a joke! After I lived in America for nearly nine years."

He smiled. "The culture shock can be jarring. I've been living in L.A. for the last four years. It's nice to meet someone else who's in the same predicament. Would you like to go down the road for a coffee?"

She froze. A man asking you out for coffee was a proposition. "I don't think so."

"Why not? Do you think your father and brothers would disapprove?"

"I'm sure they would." Her heart pounded beneath her conservative dress. Some mad reckless part of her wanted to go with him and drink that coffee. Luckily she managed to wrestle the urge under control.

"Let me at least buy you this book." He turned and headed for the shop owner. She'd forgotten all about him, ensconced in his own world in the farthest corner of the store. He showed no sign of having heard their conversation.

She wanted to protest and insist on buying the book herself, but by the time she pulled herself together the store owner was already wrapping it in brown paper and it would have been awkward. She didn't want to make a fuss.

"Thank you." She accepted the package with a pinched smile. "Perhaps I should buy you a coffee to thank you for your generous present." The book wasn't cheap. And if she were paying, it wasn't a date, right? She was twenty-seven years old. Hardly a blushing girl. She could share a coffee with a fellow English speaker to pass a dull afternoon. Her pulse accelerated as she waited for his response, torn between hoping he'd say yes, and praying that he'd say no.

"That would be very kind of you." His gaze wasn't very wolfish. He couldn't help being so handsome. Women probably misinterpreted his perfectly ordinary gestures of friendliness out of wishful thinking. She wasn't so foolish.

They stepped out into the fierce afternoon sun and walked down a long block to a row of modern shops, including a fairly new café. It had hip westernized décor, which was strangely reassuring and made her feel less like she was about to commit a massive social faux pas.

He pulled out her chair and she settled herself into it, arranging her traditional dress. Then she realized that she didn't even know his name. She glanced about, wanting to make sure no one could overhear her. The attendant was gathering menus by the bar, far enough away to be out of earshot. "I'm Daniyah…." She hesitated, her ex-husband's last name—McKay—on the tip of her tongue. She suddenly decided not to use it anymore. But using her father's last name, Hassan, which she'd given up when she married against his will, didn't feel right either. "But you can call me Dani."

"Quasar." He didn't say his surname, either. Maybe it was better that way. They were casual acquaintances, nothing more. And he was even more fearfully good-looking in real daylight, with a strong jaw and tousled hair that added to his rakish appearance.

She glanced away quickly. Her blood heated just looking at this man. "I'll have a coffee with milk."

He ordered, in expert Arabic, without looking at the

menu. "Me, too. Though I suppose we should be drinking it black, with some dates, now that we're back in Oman."

She laughed. There was something about the way he said it that made her feel like his coconspirator. "It's terrible. I find myself longing for a burrito or a foot-long sub."

"Are you going back to America soon?"

His question took her by surprise. "I don't know. I'm not sure what I'm doing." It was a relief to be honest. Maybe because he was a stranger, she felt she could let down her mask a little. "I came here in a hurry and now I seem to be becalmed."

"Becalmed?" He tilted his head and surveyed her with those striking gray-blue eyes.

"It's an old-fashioned term for a ship that's stuck out at sea because there's no wind to fill her sails." Maybe Quasar was the wind she'd been waiting for? This afternoon was already the most excitement she'd had since her arrival three months ago.

"So you need a bracing gust to set you on your way again."

"Something like that." She let the gleam in his eyes light a little spark of…something in her chest. The way he looked at her suggested that he found her attractive. Was that even possible? People used to tell her she was pretty, but her ex made her feel like the ugliest loser in the world. Right now she felt odd and frumpy in the loose dress and pants she'd worn to look modest and tasteful, but Quasar didn't even seem to notice it. He related to her as easily as if she were in her familiar jeans and T-shirt. "Why are you here?" she asked.

"Visiting my brother and his family. And trying to reconnect with my culture. I don't want to stay away too long and have my roots shrivel away." His wry grin was disarming. Just looking at him, seeing the way his white shirt and jeans showed off a powerful physique, was stirring feelings she'd almost forgotten existed.

"If you want to reconnect with your roots, you should wear a dishdasha." She could barely picture him in the long, white traditional garment, with its knotted sash and ornamental dagger at the waist.

He raised a brow. "Do you think I'd look better in one?" He was flirting.

She shrugged. "No. I'm only wearing this because I don't want to scandalize my family. I've done that enough already."

Curiosity flared in his gaze, as she'd predicted. "You don't look like the type to cause a scandal."

"Then I guess my disguise is working. I'm trying to fit in and fly under the radar."

"You're too beautiful to ever do that." He spoke softly, so the waiter couldn't hear him, but his words shocked her. She blinked at his bold flattery.

"Even traditional clothing allows your face to show," he said. "You'd have to hide that to go unnoticed."

"Or just never leave the house, which is what my father would prefer. He has no idea I'm out here right now. He thinks I'm at home writing poetry in my childhood bedroom. I'm twenty-seven and divorced, for crying out loud, and I have to sneak around like a naughty teenager."

Quasar laughed and looked as if he were going to say something, but just then the waiter brought their coffees. Dani watched Quasar's sensual mouth as he sipped his drink and she cursed the shimmer of heat that flared under her voluminous clothing.

"I think you are ready for that breeze to catch your sails," he said at last.

"I don't know what I'm ready for, to be totally honest. My divorce just became final."

He lifted his coffee cup. "Congratulations."

She giggled. "That sounds so wrong, but it does feel like something to celebrate."

"We all make mistakes. I'm thirty-one and I've never been married. That has to be a mistake of some kind. At least that's what my two happily married brothers keep insisting."

"They think you should find someone and settle down?"

"Absolutely. In fact I'm not sure they'll let me leave Oman until I'm legally wed."

She laughed. Since his brothers would not be likely to encourage him to marry a divorcée, this put them on a "friends only" footing that was rather reassuring. She could admire him without worrying that anything could come of it. But sadness trickled through her at the realization that she was damaged goods, and safely off-limits. "How do you feel about the idea?"

"Petrified." He looked rueful. "If I was cut out for marriage, I'd probably have plunged into it by now."

"You just haven't met the right person yet."

"That's what they keep telling me."

"It's better to wait for the right person than to have to extricate yourself after you've chosen the wrong one." He must have no shortage of women trailing after him. In fact two girls had sat down at a table near them and she could see them glancing over and whispering to each other.

Then again, maybe they were whispering about her. She didn't know how much had gotten out about her... situation. When she'd first arrived she assumed that no one would remember her or care what she'd been doing, but she'd forgotten what a small town Salalah could be, at least when it came to gossip.

She stiffened, and sipped her coffee. "What kind of business are you in?"

"Any kind of business that grabs my attention." His gaze stayed riveted on her face. The way he stared at her was disconcerting. She wasn't used to it. "I love to jump into a new field and be one of the first to stake out unknown territory."

"You make it sound like mountain climbing."

"Sometimes it is. Three-dimensional printing technology was my most recent fascination. Printers that can render a solid object. It's going to revolutionize manufacturing. Just imagine, you could design and print out a new pair of shoes right in your own home."

"That sounds fun."

"The technology is even being used to print human tissue for operations like skin grafts."

"Very cool."

"That's what I thought, so I invested in a start-up and helped them develop the technology. I just sold my share."

"Why? It sounds like a fascinating industry."

"I was ready to move on. Try something new."

"You're restless."

"Always."

So that's why he wasn't married. He got bored easily, then moved on to someone new and more exciting.

"What do you do?" He leaned close enough that she imagined she could smell his scent. But she couldn't. The aroma of coffee was too strong. Why was she thinking about the way he smelled? She must be attracted to him. That would explain the quickening of her pulse and the way she was growing warm all over.

This was breaking news. She didn't think she'd ever be attracted to a man again. At least that part of her was still alive, not that it was likely to do her much good.

His eyes glittered with amusement and for a frightening second she wondered if he could read her mind. "Is your occupation a secret? Do you work for the CIA?"

Her face heated. She'd been so busy noticing her brain's reaction to him that she'd forgotten he asked a question. "I'm an art historian, and most recently worked at Princeton. The ancient Near East is my area of expertise."

"Am I right in guessing that Oman counts as the Near East?"

She nodded. "It's a large area, and was the seat of many great civilizations."

"Mesopotamia, Sumer, the ziggurats at Ur-Nammu." Tiny smile lines formed at the corners of his wide, sensual mouth.

"Most people think of ancient Egypt."

"Do I sound like a show-off?"

"A little." She fought a smile. His arrogance and confidence had an effortless quality that was oddly appealing. "But I won't hold it against you."

"Thanks. You should see the museum my brother's put together. He built a hotel on the site of an old Silk Road city."

"That sounds like an art historian's nightmare."

"You'd like it! There wasn't much left, just a few stumps of walls out in the middle of an old oil field, and he's recreated it as a luxury retreat, preserving as much as possible of the original."

"Your whole family sounds rather unusual."

He laughed. "Maybe we are. We all march to our own beat. The archaeologists who excavated the site found some pottery and small figurines. You might find them interesting."

"I'm sure I would. Do you know what era they're from?"

"No clue. Maybe we can visit the place together. It's only a short drive outside Salalah. We could go tomorrow."

She froze. There was no way she could go for a drive anywhere with a total stranger. Even a seemingly handsome, charming and educated one. She didn't really know anything about him. For all she knew, he could be making everything up. And besides, her father and brothers would forbid it. "I can't."

"Maybe another time, then. Let me give you my phone number."

She glanced at the two girls at the nearby table. Their dark eyes were still darting to her and her companion. They'd be sure to notice. But what harm could come of it if she never called him?

Her heart pounded while she watched him write the number in an assured hand on the back of the blue paper napkin. "I'm staying at my brother's hotel here in Salalah. It's right on the beach. Where do you live?"

She swallowed. This was getting dangerously personal. "Not far." No one knew she was here, which was by design. "I really should be getting back." She shoved the napkin into her pocket.

"I'll walk you home."

"Oh, no. There's no need. You stay here and relax." She put down some cash to pay for the coffee. He thrust it back to her with a shocked expression, and she decided—once again—to avoid a scene by accepting his hospitality. "Thanks for the coffee." He rose when she did and for a split second she had an insane thought he might try to kiss her. Her whole body braced as adrenaline rushed through her. Then he thrust out his hand and she shook it. "And thanks for the book."

"Call me. I'd like to go see the artifacts with you."

She picked up her new book, then turned and walked out of the café as fast as she could. Most likely the tension and excitement was all in her head—and her body—but she couldn't be sure. Either way, it was exhilarating and she felt more alive than she had in months. Years, even. And all because of a man she had no business even talking to.

She walked home quickly. Her dad wouldn't get home for a while but she wanted to arrive before her brothers came back from their respective schools. Her younger brother, Khalid, usually came straight home to do his homework, but her older brother, Jalil, often stayed late in the technical college library to pore over the designs for his latest engineering project. She liked to make them a snack before they returned, but today she wouldn't have time. In fact she barely had time to put her new book in her bedroom and shove the napkin with Quasar's number into a drawer before the front door opened and Khalid crashed in and flung his book bag down in the hallway before heading into the kitchen.

"I took a nap," she fibbed, as her brother's eyes scanned the empty kitchen counters. Maybe they were growing too dependent on her. She didn't plan to be here forever.

"A nap? In the middle of the day? You're going soft."

What would he say if she revealed that she'd let a strange man buy her a book—and a coffee? He'd probably question her sanity.

She read her new book for a while before she heard her father's distinctive rap on the door. Even though the door was open he liked someone to let him in. She pulled back the latch, forcing a bright smile. "Hello, Father." She kissed his cheek. As usual he brushed it off as if she were a fly. "How was your day?"

"Same as usual." His gruff voice and glum expression rarely softened. "Too many fools in this business. Always looking for new cheaper ways to do things that have worked just fine for decades." An engineer, he was often irritated by new technologies and methods. He asked her brother about his schoolwork, as usual. He never asked her about her day, which was a plus today since she couldn't have said anything truthful about it.

"Help Faizal prepare an excellent supper tonight, dear." Faizal was the cook who came over to make dinner every night. Her father fixed his beady gaze on her. "A friend of mine will be joining us." He looked her up and down in a way that made her stomach muscles clench.

"That's great. Is he a friend from work?"

"Not from the firm, no. He's a supplier. Rivets and nuts." He squinted at her for a moment. "Wear a color that suits your complexion more."

She glanced down at the navy blue she'd worn all day. "Why?"

"That blue is rather draining on you. Something brighter would be more attractive."

Dani stood speechless. This was the first time her father had expressed an opinion on her clothes. Was he planning to set her up with his friend? She wanted to ask but didn't dare.

She'd assumed he saw her as such a social pariah that it wouldn't be worth the bother of trying to marry her off again. Maybe he'd grown tired of having her under his roof and hoped to find someone who would take her off his hands. She hurried to her room, wondering if she could find an even less flattering color to wear.

Quasar hadn't thought she looked washed out in the blue. The way he'd looked at her had made her feel as if she'd been glowing like a spring flower. His daring gaze made her feel desirable—and it made her feel desire. The memory of it made her blood hum.

Alone in her room she let herself dream about him for a moment. What would it be like to accompany him to his brother's hotel/museum or whatever it was? People had said her ex-husband was good-looking—she'd thought so herself until she grew to understand his true character—but he had nothing on Quasar's dramatic features and playful charm.

Of course, the man she'd just met was undoubtedly used to women drooling over him. He was probably shocked that she refused his suggestion that they meet again. If she were in America, without traditional rules to consider, would she have said yes?

No. She had to be honest. She wouldn't have accepted an invitation from a strange man who gave every impression of being a playboy dilettante of the worst kind. Let him go charm someone else into making a fool of herself with him. Dani Hassan wasn't making any more mistakes in the man department.

Changing into a dark forest-green dress with silver edging, she went back to the kitchen to help the cook prepare a traditional chicken dish with rice and vegetables. She wasn't sure how the elderly Faizal felt about her assistance—Dani suspected he'd just as soon she butt out and leave him to his business—but joining him in the kitchen gave her an activity to look forward to, when there was precious little to do around the house all day.

She arranged the meal in the dining room, on the carpeted floor, Omani style, with more attention to detail than usual—artfully folded napkins, the prettier glasses—and waited with grim curiosity for her father's "friend" to arrive. When he finally did, she hung back and waited in her room with headphones on, pretending to listen to music, until her brothers had been introduced and one of them was sent for her. The sight of her prospective beau made her heart sink.

"Daniyah, I'm delighted to introduce you to Mr. Samir Al Kabisi." He was at least sixty, with thinning gray hair combed over a freckled scalp and a bulbous nose like a misshapen potato. His eyes were yellowish and his teeth crooked as he spoke the traditional greeting.

He didn't extend his hand, so she bowed her head and attempted a smile. Did her dad seriously consider this man a potential partner for her? He must have a very low opinion of her worth.

On the other hand, maybe she had too high an opinion of herself. She didn't know this man at all. He could be perfectly nice and here she was judging him entirely on his looks—or lack of them. Wouldn't a kind and sensible man with a homely appearance be better than a gorgeous and dashing jerk?

She'd prefer the company of a good book.

"Do come in and have some coffee." She kept her smile fixed while she served the fragrant hot drink in the ornate brass urn they kept for visitors. Her father engaged their guest in riveting conversation about the nuts and rivets industry, and he responded with brief comments in the rasp of a heavy smoker.

Dani wished she could go hide in her room. They stumbled through dinner with innocuous conversation about the city and a recent burst of new construction. After dinner her father leaned forward and pinned her with his gaze. "Mr. Al Kabisi was widowed seven years ago."

"I'm so sorry for your loss." Uh-oh. Seemed like her father was finally getting to the point.

"He's mourned his wife for many years but I've persuaded him that perhaps it is time to set the shroud of grief aside."

Dani swallowed.

"Boys, come out into the garden with me for a few minutes." Her brothers looked perplexed for a moment, especially Khalid, who probably wanted to go play with his Xbox, but they got with the program and followed her dad out of the room.

Alone in the room with this man more than twice her age, Dani had no idea what to say. He stood and cleared his throat. "I see no shame in a woman divorcing a man who is cruel to her."

Her heart clenched. He must know her humiliating story. "That's kind of you." Now what was she supposed to say? She did see considerable shame in marrying a man old enough to be her father, whom she had less than nothing in common with, out of desperation. And she had no intention of doing so.

"I own my own business and my house. My three sons live and work in Muscat with their families, so I am all alone here. My income is—"

A desperate need to interrupt his sales pitch overcame her and she rose to her feet. "You're very kind but I really don't think—"

He rose, too, with considerable difficulty since they were sitting on the floor. His eyes bulged. "I am still potent." His fetid breath stung her nostrils. "So have no fear that you will be neglected."

Her dinner churned in her stomach. "I'm not ready to marry again. It's too soon. I'm still…recovering." She'd

be in permanent recovery if this were the kind of prospect available to her.

At that exact moment she resolved to throw caution to
the wind and take Quasar up on his invitation.

Two

Quasar emerged from the warm water of the pool with chlorine-blurred eyes. Sun shone on the sandstone surfaces of the elegant hotel buildings, and a light breeze ruffled the rows of majestic palm trees.

"Your phone's ringing," Celia, his brother Salim's wife, called from beside the pool, where she was relaxing with Sara, the wife of his brother Elan. They'd just eaten a leisurely poolside breakfast and were planning a day of relaxation on the nearby beach. Quasar was soaking wet and bouncing his three-year-old niece, Hannah, on his shoulders. "I doubt it's anything important. I'm taking a break from business."

"Throw me!" Little Hannah could yell surprisingly loud for such a small human.

"I can't. You can't swim." She'd watched him tossing her cousin and was desperate to join in the fun. He ducked down and almost dunked her, then rose up fast, making her scream.

"You're so good with kids. You should have some." Sara sipped her nonalcoholic cocktail. She was pregnant with her third child.

"Nonsense. I just need to spend more time with you guys. I think this is the first time we've all been together since Salim's wedding. I'm not going to let that happen again."

Salim and Celia lived in Salalah, with their children Kira and Basia. This hotel was the headquarters for his chain of luxurious resorts throughout the region. Elan and Sara lived in Nevada, where they ran their thriving fuel exploration business while raising Hannah and their son, Ben. Quasar was usually jetting around cooking up projects and it was rare for them all to make the time to relax. For the last decade he'd been so busy starting businesses and partying hard that he hadn't had time to get bored. Now he was beginning to think he'd missed out on something. Something big.

He didn't even have a permanent address right now. He'd sold his L.A. penthouse for a profit too good to refuse, and his worldly goods were in a storage unit near Hollywood. He'd recently bought a farmhouse in the hills near Salalah, but it had needed months of renovation so he'd barely spent any time there.

"It's ringing again." Celia peered at his phone, which sat on the table next to her. "Same number. Want me to get it for you?"

"Okay."

She picked up his phone. "Quasar's phone. Celia speaking." Then she frowned. "They hung up." She lifted a brow. "I hope I didn't scare off one of your girlfriends."

He swung his niece around until she shrieked loud enough to pierce his eardrums. "I don't have any girlfriends." Then he froze.

Dani.

What if she'd decided to call him, and now a woman answered his phone? "Let's go dry you off, kid." He carried his niece to the steps and climbed out, dripping onto the sandstone tiles. He dried his hands on his towel and snatched up his phone.

Celia leaned toward Sara. "I think he does have a girl-friend or two that he's worried about."

He didn't recognize the number, but it looked local. He called it, and listened while it rang.

"Hello?" a shy, thin voice answered.

"This is Quasar. You just called my phone." He didn't want to say her name in case it wasn't her. He'd made that mistake before.

"Hi. It's Dani." She hesitated, possibly wondering about the woman who'd answered his phone.

"I'm so glad you called." He walked along the edge of the pool, away from his sisters-in-law. He could feel their eyes on him. "I was hoping you would. That was my sister-in-law Celia who answered."

"Oh." She sounded relieved. "I'd like to go see the museum pieces with you, if you're still interested."

"Absolutely. Is this afternoon good?" He didn't want to wait and take a chance that she'd change her mind.

"Okay."

"Excellent. If you give me your address, I'll come pick you up."

She told him that she preferred to meet him outside the vegetable stalls at the end of the street with the café. Apparently she didn't want him coming to her house. And she had to be home by four, at the latest. It was all starting to sound intriguingly cloak-and-dagger.

"Sure, I'll be there at noon." His blood pumped a little faster at the prospect of seeing her again. He wondered if she'd wear the elegant traditional attire she'd had on yesterday, or something more Western. He was curious about her figure. He could already tell she was slim, but he had no idea about the cut of her hips, the shape of her legs, or the curve of her bosom. There was something to be said for that kind of mystery.

Still, he promised himself that he wasn't going to make even the slightest hint of a move on her unless she showed signs of strong interest. He was a guest here in Oman and although he didn't remember too much about the local customs, he knew that toying with a woman's affections was a total no-no.

Unfortunately that didn't dampen his enthusiasm one bit.

"Did I hear you say that you're meeting someone this afternoon?" Sara asked. She was smoothing sunblock on her arm. "I thought we were doing a barbecue on the beach."

"Something came up." He tried not to reveal his excitement.

His willowy sister-in-law Celia tilted her head. "Is she very beautiful?"

"How do you know it's not a dull business meeting?" He rubbed himself with the towel.

"The look in your eyes." She smiled, but raised one of her slender brows, too. "Those dangerous blue eyes where a woman is likely to drown in passion."

"I suspect most women are better swimmers than you think." He swatted six-year-old Ben with a towel as he ran by. "And as it happens I'm taking her to see the restored oasis that you created." Celia had first come to Oman as the landscape designer for the project. "She's a historian specializing in this region so I think she'll be interested in the artifacts you found."

"I bet she will. Something tells me you don't want to turn this into a family expedition where we all meet her."

He smiled. "Not yet. I only just met her myself. I don't want to scare her off."

"Very sensible. Though maybe she should be a little scared. The press coverage from your latest shenanigans hasn't even died down yet. Laura was creating a stir on Twitter this morning talking about her broken heart."

Ouch. Meeting Dani had shoved his most recent girlfriend out of his mind. Unfortunately she was still in a lot of other people's minds since she was a well-known actress with a talent for self-promotion. "I promise I didn't really break her heart. She broke it all by herself. She's one of those people who are in love with an impossible ideal of love. I don't think anyone could make her happy."

"In love with love?" Celia laughed.

Sara wandered over and sat down next to Celia on one of the elegant cushioned chaises that surrounded the pool. The shade of a nearby palm tree kept the sun off her face as she settled in. "Who's in love?"

"Everyone's in love with Quasar. It's very trying for him."

Sara shrugged and pulled off her T-shirt to reveal a turquoise bikini. "Not me. I'm still in love with Elan."

Quasar draped his towel over the back of a chair and flexed his shoulders until they cracked. "And so you should be. He's much more reliable than me." His stolid, workaholic brother had hired Sara as his secretary and was suitably appalled when he fell in love with her.

"Nor me. I still love Salim." Celia said it while looking at her husband, his oldest brother, who, incongruously dressed in a dark gray pinstripe suit, had just walked up to her and kissed her on the cheek.

Quasar watched in mock amazement. "We can tell. I never would have thought I'd see the mighty Salim indulge in public displays of affection."

"The right woman can transform any one of us. Most likely when we least expect it." Salim spoke with the quiet assurance of a prophet, his arms draped around his beautiful wife's neck. "Even you."

Quasar laughed. "Don't be so sure."

"He has a date this afternoon," Celia said into her husband's ear.

Salim straightened up. "Tell me she's kidding."

"It's nothing to worry about. We both spoke English so we struck up a conversation."

"Where?" Salim's dark, penetrating eyes narrowed. Quasar drew himself taller under their accusing stare.

"A local bookshop."

Salim stared at him while Elan jogged up, looking muscular and athletic as usual. "Quasar is the only man I know who can go out to buy a book and come back with a woman. Even in Oman."

"I hardly came back with her in my pocket. She was interesting, that's all. I have no intention of indulging in anything but conversation with her."

Elan laughed. "I'm sure you've said that before."

"Have a little faith in me." Quasar grabbed Kira, Salim and Celia's oldest, around the waist and swung her up onto his shoulders. "Kira has faith in me, don't you?"

"What's faith?" Kira lisped both words, looking confused.

"When you believe in something without having actual proof."

Kira stared at him for a moment. "Like a fairy."

"Yes. Like a fairy."

Kira pushed her lip out. "I don't believe in fairies."

Quasar couldn't help laughing as he set her down. "Thanks for nothing."

Salim crossed his arms, looking sensible and invincible as ever in his suit. "Well said, Kira. An Al Mansur prefers some empirical evidence." His stern features softened. "Would you like to come help Daddy in the office? I have some papers that need coloring in."

"Yes please!"

Quasar stared after Salim and Kira, shaking his head, as his *über*-serious older brother walked off, hand in hand with the little girl he hadn't even known existed until she was two.

"I've never seen Salim so happy. Nor you, Elan."

"We've shared our secrets, brother. It's all about finding the right woman."

"And managing not to fire her or drive her away." Sara winked.

Quasar thought for a moment. "There's a theme here. You and Celia were both working for my brothers. Maybe I need to hire someone," he teased.

Sara cocked her head. "And get her pregnant by mistake. Don't forget that happened to both of us, as well."

"At least that's one thing I can't be accused of."

"Yet," said Celia, smoothing sunblock onto her long legs with a wry smile. "Be careful. Obviously Al Mansur men are very potent."

"Like I said, we're just going to talk. She's an Omani. There's no question of us getting naked without elaborate negotiations involving goats and camels."

"That's a relief, then." Celia leaned toward him and whispered. "Still, take a condom with you."

"Sister, you shock me."

She patted his arm. "Just speaking from experience."

Dani arrived at the fruit-and-vegetable market a full ten minutes before noon. She didn't want to take a chance of getting held up and missing their meeting. She busied herself looking over the stalls full of fragrant limes, garlic and bright piles of carrots. Young children darted around their mother's legs, making a game of tagging each other with their blue plastic shopping bags. She was trying to look busy testing the freshness of oranges at a citrus stall when something told her to look up.

Her gaze fell on Quasar, striding along the dusty street, chin high, gaze fixed intently on her. Dressed in white linen pants and shirt, he looked as cool and fresh as a tall glass of water.

She braced herself, hoping he wouldn't draw attention to them by calling out her name. She put down the orange and walked to meet him, keeping her gaze averted.

Luckily he was discreet. "Good afternoon," he said quietly. Her eyes wandered to his lips, and imagined them kissing her hello. Which mercifully didn't happen.

"Good afternoon. Almost afternoon. We're both early." Her heart fluttered with excitement, which was silly since she barely knew this man. The sun had kissed his skin a shade darker since yesterday, making his incongruous blue eyes shine even brighter. Even white teeth glittered in his wolfish smile. He looked like trouble. If she had any sense she'd make up an excuse and run for home right now.

But she didn't.

"My car is parked around the corner." He seemed as if he were about to thread his arm through hers, or put his hand at her waist, but he hesitated, aware of the conservative local customs. The unmade gesture ratcheted up the tension between them. Her body hummed with both the desire to be touched and the fear of it. She walked beside him self-consciously as he led her to a silver Mercedes, already covered in a fine film of inevitable dust, and opened the passenger door for her. "I'm so glad you're coming out to the resort. I haven't been there since my brother Salim's wedding."

"I bet it was spectacular."

"Oh, it was. Salim doesn't do anything by halves."

"I bet you don't, either." She snuck a glance at his bold profile as he pulled out onto the road.

"I do tend to throw myself into things."

"Until you grow bored with them." She regretted the words as soon as she'd said them. It sounded like she was scolding him. "I'm sorry. I shouldn't have said that."

"Except that you're right." He shone those fierce blue eyes on her. "I have been accused of having a short attention span. I prefer to think that there are just so many things to do that I can only devote so much time to each one."

No doubt he felt the same way about women. He could never pursue a proper relationship with her since she was a divorcée and wouldn't meet his obviously demanding brothers' criteria for wife material. On the other hand, he might have no qualms about having an affair with her. She had to be careful to resist his charms.

They drove through a cultivated grove of date palms, then out of the city into the desert. She snuck furtive glances at him while he drove, taking in the sharp cut of his aristocratic features, and the sensual curve of his mouth. Resisting his charms might take some doing and she'd better take the resisting seriously since her heart was still in repair mode from her one and only serious relationship. The last thing she needed was to get it bruised or broken again by this man.

She resolved to keep her eyes focused out the window. The desert landscape was hypnotically minimalist, with its subtle colors and bold blue sky. The fog-shrouded mountains rose up ahead of them, and the landscape changed dramatically as they drove up into the lush green oasis of plant and bird life that made Salalah a tourist destination during the annual rainy season. Right now it was June, dry and sunny, in between the spring rains and the summer downpours that got underway in July.

Quasar kept the conversation rolling with no apparent effort. They chattered about the lifestyle differences between Oman and America, and the bond deepened between them as they agreed that it was hard to move from one country to the other without severe culture shock.

"So you haven't really lived in Oman at all."

"I haven't lived here permanently since my mom died. My dad packed Elan and me off to boarding school overseas. I was young enough to adapt easily. I never really looked back."

"You didn't miss your family."

"I didn't miss my father. He was very strict and kind of mean. I guess I'm not the type to get hung up looking for Daddy's approval. I made friends and moved on."

"And you've been moving on ever since."

He turned to her. "You think my nomadic lifestyle is the result of childhood psychological trauma?" He sounded serious, but she saw a twinkle in his eye.

She shrugged. "I don't know." She wondered what depths lay beneath his cocky exterior. Was there a wounded little boy craving approval and love? "Where is home for you?"

He shot her a glance with those piercing blue eyes. "Good question. Until recently it was L.A., but I just sold my condo there. Right now the only place I own is a house out in the desert here. I don't know if I'd call it home since I just had it renovated, but I bought it as a place to put down some roots and reconnect with my heritage, so maybe I'm heading in the right direction."

"Or the wrong direction." She laughed. "Do you really think Oman is your home now, or are you more comfortable in the United States? I feel more of a stranger here these days than I did in New Jersey. Moving around the world hasn't made my life easier."

"How did you end up in America when your family is still here?"

"My story's not so different from yours. I was sent to live with my aunt in New Jersey when my mother died. The idea was that I would go to college there then come back and work in my father's engineering firm while pursuing a suitable husband. I don't think it occurred to my father that I could just switch majors and stay there."

"Did he mind?"

"He went ballistic when I told him I wasn't coming back to Oman. It took me a long time to pluck up the courage to admit that I'd majored in art history instead of engineering. Since I paid the bill myself with an inheritance from my mom he didn't find out until it was too late."

She saw a smile tilt the edge of Quasar's mouth. "So you're a bit of a rebel."

"Only a very tiny bit."

"I wonder." He gave her a mysterious look.

She had been a rebel in choosing to chart her own course in life. The fact that she'd been blown right off it and ended up back here again made her wonder about her choices. She planned on sticking closer to the straight and narrow from now on. A degree in engineering certainly would present a lot more employment opportunities than her currently useless art history Ph.D.

"We're nearly there. It's called Saliyah, after my sister-in-law Celia, who designed the grounds and ensnared the heart of my brother Salim."

"That's so romantic." They turned on to a side road in

the desert. Spreading date palms cropped up to line the desolate road and cast lush shade over its dusty surface.

She gasped at the sight of a large animal underneath a nearby tree. "Look, a camel."

Quasar laughed. "Salim's always complaining about them. They eat his expensive landscaping. I figure he should just consider them part of the scenery and worth supporting. This place has been attracting a lot of visitors from overseas and they eat that stuff up."

The road led up to a high mud-brick wall with an elaborately carved arch. They entered and drove around a large circular fountain, where moving water sparkled like diamonds in the hot midday sun. Quasar helped her out of the car and it was whisked away by a valet while she blinked and adjusted to the bright light. They walked across a smooth courtyard of inlaid sandstone into a shady lobby that looked like the throne room of an ancient palace. Colorful mosaics covered the walls and lush seating arrangements were clustered around impressive botanical specimens. The guests were an interesting mix of glamorous Omanis and other Arabs, their traditional garb accented with Chanel sunglasses and Fendi handbags, and chic Europeans showing a lot of carefully suntanned skin. Waiters served coffee and dates, and the scent of rose petals filled the air.

"Would you like some coffee, or do you want to get right to the good stuff?"

She glanced about, feeling awkward and out of place. She didn't belong here among these stylish and confident members of the international elite. "I'd like to see the museum."

"I suspected you would." He shot her a smile that made her blood pump faster. "Follow me." She walked across the elegant foyer, trying to keep her eyes from tracking the lithe roll of his hips in too obvious a manner.

Sexual magnetism radiated from him like an exotic scent. Women's eyes swiveled to him from all directions, and it was all she could do not to glare at them. As if he were even hers to be jealous about! She felt their critical gaze on her, too. No doubt they wondered what a fine specimen of manhood like Quasar was doing with a mousy nobody like her.

Quasar led her out through a grand arch into a formal garden with a trickling fountain. Romantic-looking couples sat on upholstered sofas, chatting under the shade of the exotic plants. For an instant she imagined sitting there with him, just enjoying the afternoon. But he would hardly romance her in front of the employees at his brother's hotel.

Was he attracted to her? It was hard to imagine that someone like Quasar, whom almost any woman—including the wealthy, beautiful, famous and brilliant—would find desirable, would be interested in her. But if he weren't, why did he invite her here?

Quasar waited for her to pass him when they reached the path to the museum, but she hesitated, uncertain. "This is it." He gestured at the carved wood door, almost hidden by flowering bushes.

Dani peered at the door with a sparkle of excitement in her eyes. Today she wore a traditional Omani getup in a rose shade that brought out the roses in her cheeks and lips. He hadn't noticed yesterday what a mobile and sensual mouth she had. "It's almost as if they didn't want people to discover the treasures inside."

"Maybe they don't. I suspect they're more interested

in selling them expensive massages." He smiled. "Let's see if it's open."

He tried the handle. She played with her headscarf, almost nervous. What was she afraid of? Being alone with him in a cool, darkened room filled with antiques?

Hmm. If she knew his reputation she'd do well to be afraid. But she couldn't know anything about him. They hadn't exchanged last names.

He tried the brass handle and the door creaked open, sending a rush of air-conditioned air toward them.

The room was dimly lit, with spotlights shining down on a few key pieces, mostly ornately carved silver.

She walked right past those to some dull-colored pots displayed on a shelf against the far wall. "These are ancient," she breathed, and she rushed forward to examine the closest one. "Two thousand years old at least. Back when this area was a pit stop along the Silk Road."

The same color as the mud-brick walls, the pottery didn't look that exciting to Quasar. Still, Dani's exuberance was contagious.

"Everything here was found buried beneath the sand at the site. Celia says the oasis was in use for thousands of years."

"Camel trains would come through Salalah before making the long trek up through the desert toward Jerusalem." Dani wheeled around, and headed for a display case filled with silver jewelry. "Look at these pieces. They're exquisite."

He examined the big heavy silver bracelets and necklaces that were large enough to strangle a camel. "I bet they're heavy."

"I bet they're not." She smiled at him. "Some of them are hollow. You could store prayers in them for protection. Look at the carving on this one. It must have taken the craftsman weeks to make all those intricate designs." She sighed. "We're too busy these days to make anything so beautiful."

"How come you don't wear jewelry if you admire it so much?" He noticed for the first time that her ears were pierced, but unadorned by earrings.

"You don't wear jewelry when you're trying to disappear." She flashed him a wry smile. "The ladies wearing these pieces wanted everyone to notice them."

"And to gossip about how rich their daddies or husbands were, I suspect."

"Absolutely." She grinned. "I bet they enjoyed it, though."

She moved over to a display of colorful clothing. "These aren't antique."

"Nope. Celia thought it would be a good idea to include them to celebrate our traditional clothing. Hardly anyone wears such bright colors these days."

"They wanted to stand out against the dusty backdrop of the desert, like magnificent exotic birds. Maybe I should start wearing stuff like this myself?" She lifted a brow.

He laughed. "I can't picture you in something that loud."

"Me, either." She sighed. "Truth be told, I prefer to disappear into the scenery. I suppose I always have."

"Even before you were married?" He burned with curiosity to know more about her marriage, but didn't want to jump the gun and scare her off by asking too much.

She nodded. "I guess I'm a wallflower at heart."

"You could never hide against a wall, even though your dress today is a similar color to this rosy clay." He picked up the end of her scarf and felt the soft fabric between thumb and finger. Desire stirred in him as he imagined lifting more of the fabric to discover what lay beneath.

Her breath quickened and he thought he saw her pupils dilate a little. The attraction between them was definitely mutual. She turned from him and hurried over to a shelf with a display of big brass serving platters. To him they looked like something he could buy in the souk this afternoon if he wanted. She seemed riveted by one of them, though. He moved right behind her, so he could almost feel the heat of her body in the cool air. She peered at the largest dish. "What a pretty scene. It looks like the Dhofar mountains. It's quite unusual to depict something representational in the post-Islamic era—"

She turned to him, that glorious mouth still talking, and he fought an almost unbearable urge to kiss her.

He managed not to, though. Desire raced through him like fire along a line of gasoline and he tried hard to fight it back. *You just met her. You don't know her.*

Heck, that had never stopped him before. The best way to get to know a girl was to become intimate right away. Let the chemistry mingle and see what kind of explosions happened.

Not this girl, though. Dani had been hurt, and he didn't know the details. She was recovering from a bad marriage and the last thing she needed was to be seduced by a roving stranger who was only in town for a couple of weeks.

Well, he didn't know how long he'd be here, but it wouldn't be long. He was just visiting family and trying to figure out what to do next.

And all he wanted to do right now was kiss Dani.

Mercifully she'd moved away, and was examining a series of *khanjar* daggers hanging on the wall. Most of the sheaths were ornately carved silver, but she was bent over the least elaborate one. "This must be camel leather and camel bone. I suppose this is what they all looked like many centuries ago, when people carried them for use, not for ornamentation."

Keep your dagger sheathed, he commanded himself.

"Why are you smiling?"

"I told my brother I wouldn't indulge in anything but conversation with you today. And I was just thinking that you're making it very difficult." He was nothing if not honest.

She looked startled for a moment, then regained her composure. "Why did you tell your brother that?"

"He's worried about me embarking on an unsuitable romance. He doesn't trust my judgment."

"You'd better keep your distance. As an Omani he's not going to approve of me since I'm divorced, so you can go ahead and think of me as off-limits."

"What if that just makes me want you more?"

"Then you're incorrigible."

"You wouldn't be the first to call me that. Actually you might. That's a pretty unusual word. *Impossible* is a more popular choice."

A smile tugged at the edges of her mouth. "An impossible man is the very last thing I need, so I think we can mutually agree to be platonic."

"Speak for yourself."

"I think I just did." She smiled and walked quietly over to a display of large, ornate coffeepots.

Dani wasn't playing hard to get. She *was* hard to get. In fact kissing her might take the same amount of effort required to climb Mount Kilimanjaro. On the other hand, it might well be worth it, and he did enjoy a challenge.

Three

How could a simple glance get her excited? Especially from someone who was an obvious playboy. He wouldn't be this confident and flirtatious if he weren't. He was exactly the kind of man she needed to stay away from. She shouldn't be here at all. And when she looked at her watch, she realized she'd be lucky if she got back home in time. "I really do have to get back to Salalah now." They'd been browsing in the museum for nearly two hours. She'd endured many exciting brushes against him as he leaned over a new oil jar or polished brass mirror to get a closer look. His scent filled her senses like an intoxicating drug. It was lucky he hadn't made a move on her as she wasn't at all sure how she'd react.

Like a junkie, probably.

"Of course. Let's go." He pushed the door open from behind her. "I have to admit that I thought of this stuff as a bunch of old junk last time I was here, but seeing the pieces through your eyes brings them back to life."

Seeing herself through his eyes was bringing her back to life. When Quasar looked at her she almost felt as if he could see right through her billowing traditional attire to her body beneath. Her skin hummed with awareness of his interest in her. The desire racing along her veins shocked her, when she'd been so sure she'd never feel it again.

"I'd love to learn more about the history of the site." She tried to distract herself from the mysterious sensations tingling in her blood. To focus on the unusual townlike layout of the resort, with its central oasis and native plantings.

"You need to talk to my sister-in-law—Celia. I know she did some research in order to plan the landscaping."

Dani swallowed. She couldn't imagine that he'd really introduce her to his family. They'd be bound to disapprove of her.

Quasar led her past the bubbling fountain and back through the spacious, open hotel lobby.

"What a lovely place."

"Very profitable, too, apparently. It got recommended in *Condé Nast Traveler* almost as soon as it opened and it's been booked solid ever since."

"Tourism will be good for the Omani economy. It's important to diversify. The oil won't last forever."

"Too true. I should probably be paying more attention to business opportunities while I'm here. Usually that's foremost on my mind, but I seem to be a little distracted." His flashing glance made something ripple inside her.

A valet had Quasar's car ready before they even reached the main entrance. Quasar opened the door for her himself, a thoughtful gesture that touched her. She told him about her Ph.D. thesis as they sped back across the desert.

"Persian painting, huh? Aren't some of those erotic?"

"Absolutely. Some were even intended as instruction in the art of lovemaking."

"Have you tried following the instructions?"

She laughed. "No. That would not have been my ex-husband's style at all. He didn't like being told what to do." Sex with Gordon had been very wham-bam-thank-you-ma'am. At first she'd enjoyed it anyway for the sheer physical pleasure and the emotional connection she thought she'd felt. Later it had become just another wearing encounter with him that she wanted to avoid.

"I wonder if it's worth attempting."

"If what is?" She'd got lost in unhappy memories about her marriage, staring through the windshield at the bare, brown desert.

"Following the advice in the erotic paintings." He shot a dangerous glance that made her stomach quiver.

"I suppose there's only one way to find out." She lifted a brow.

"Is that an invitation?" She saw that smile tug at his mouth.

"Not even slightly." Her body begged to differ. In fact he had quite literally brought her dormant libido back to life. She didn't think she'd ever be attracted to a man again after the depressing downward spiral of her only serious relationship. For two years now she'd felt nothing, until Quasar had looked at her in that bookshop. As they talked, she'd sensed her body literally switching back on, like an electrical circuit that had been disconnected for a while and was now plugged back in so current could flow through it. Right now it was flowing to all kinds of nooks and crannies she'd all but forgotten.

She watched his long, elegant fingers resting on the wheel, and wondered what they'd feel like on her skin. Good thing she was too sensible to find out. Her reputation was already in tatters and she certainly wasn't going to rush headlong into another unsuitable relationship. A glance at the dashboard clock made her nervous. "Will we really be back by four?"

She felt the car surge forward as he accelerated. "If it can be done, I'll do it."

"Let me guess, that's your personal motto."

He flashed those slate-blue eyes at her. "You're not so far wrong. Lately I've been thinking it might be time for me to slow down, though. There may be some things I can leave undone."

Like seducing me. "You plan to become more selective as you mature."

"Exactly. At this point I think I should focus on only the very best."

"Business opportunities?"

He took his eyes off the road again and kept them on hers for far too long. After an agonizing interval that heated her blood almost to the boiling point, she glanced nervously out the windshield, half afraid they'd driven right off the narrow strip of tarmac.

"Among other things." When he finally looked back at the long, empty road—not a moment too soon—her heart was pounding and her lips parted. The effect he had on her was a little frightening.

"But how do you know something is the very best until you try it?" She wanted to fill the air with conversation. Right now the thoughts in her brain and the sensations in her body were making her very uncomfortable.

"I have a lifetime of experience. Enough to be something of a connoisseur." He spoke softly, and glanced at her quickly this time. Just long enough to convince her that he was completely serious.

She believed him. The desert swept past, and they climbed into the lush mountains again. She let out a breath she didn't realize she'd been holding. "I can't believe how beautiful it is up here. This is the first time

I've come to the mountains in years. My dad and brothers have no interest in nature."

"Let's come back tomorrow." He said it casually, and didn't even look at her. "I'll bring some binoculars and we can look for birds."

No. Just say no. You can't do this. Going out with a strange man a second time—or would it be the third, if she counted that cup of coffee?—would confirm that they were having some kind of…relationship. She wouldn't call it an affair since there was nothing sensual or romantic about it, except in her mind.

Her mouth wouldn't form the simple rejection. If she said no she'd probably never see Quasar again. That would be very sensible but the prospect was too depressing to contemplate. There'd be nothing but dull days at home, cooking the same familiar dinners, tidying her bare room, broken up with occasional walks to the bookshop and the fruit stalls. Possibly a frighteningly unattractive suitor would take pity on her from time to time. Since she didn't have any kind of promising escape plan, who knew how long that might go on for? "Okay."

He turned to her with an expression of surprise.

"You thought I'd say no."

"I did."

She loved that he didn't lie. "Apparently I'm more reckless than you thought."

"I like that in a woman." His wicked grin hinted at trouble to come. And strangely enough, she was starting to look forward to it.

The next morning she dressed in jeans and a T-shirt. Considering she'd worn little else for all her years in the United States, it was odd how daring it felt to don them. When she returned, her father had told her she should wear conservative clothing and conduct herself like an Omani woman, and—grateful for the chance to stay here—she'd obeyed. They were only clothes, right? She quickly adapted to covering her arms and legs, and her hair—the way she'd been taught as a child.

But dressing in Western clothing again was liberating and felt right. She did don a cover-up and headscarf before Quasar showed up, but she shed them in the car with relief and enjoyed Quasar's admiring gaze on her body-hugging jeans and T-shirt.

Driving up into the lush green mountains with a handsome man, Dani felt a sense that anything was possible, something she hadn't experienced since her college days. They parked and walked along a wooded trail as thick with leaves and scents and life as any trail in the New Jersey woodlands. It amazed her that during this season, paradise existed right here in her arid homeland. In a way it proved that anything was possible—anywhere—with a little rain and mist to break up the relentless heat and sun that scorched most of Oman into a virtual wasteland.

"A steppe eagle." Quasar stopped and grabbed her arm. He pointed high in a tree where a magnificent bird looked posed, as if it sat on an ancient Egyptian frieze. "It's seen something."

The bird stayed frozen for a few moments, then dropped like a rock toward land, before swooping up on broad, flapping wings with some small creature in its mouth.

"It caught its prey. What a magnificent sight." Dani peered after it as it perched on a branch nearby. "Though I can't help but feel bad for the animal that's about to be eaten."

"Eat or be eaten." Quasar's grip on her arm had softened into a sort of caress. "It's the way of the world."

His touch heated her skin. She was usually the one being eaten. "Do you really believe that? Isn't there any middle ground?"

He looked amused. "I suppose so. I haven't explored it myself."

"Since I can't imagine you being eaten, then I assume you're used to being the one doing the devouring."

He laughed. "Too right. I used to keep a falcon for hunting. Trained it myself. I'd spend hours out here tracking prey with it when I was a kid." She shrank a little from his touch. His admitted predatory attitude should make her wary. "But don't be afraid. I won't eat you."

"No?" She looked up into his face. His dark blue eyes were soft, curious.

"No." The high midday sun illuminated his aristocratic features. Of course he wouldn't be interested in devouring her. Obviously she'd been out of circulation too long to think that a man as magnificent and confident as Quasar would be interested in her.

"Maybe just a tiny bite." His wide, sensual mouth hitched slightly. Something strange was happening in her belly. It was the way he looked at her, like he held her in his grasp. She couldn't look away. His face was moving closer, his sparkling eyes still fixed right on hers. She could smell his musky, masculine scent. Any minute now she'd feel the roughness of his skin....

His lips met hers in a rush, like the eagle falling on its prey. Far from diving for cover, her mouth rose to his and melded with it. Sensation crashed over her. She was dimly aware of their natural surroundings—the wind in the trees, animals scurrying nearby—and of his hands resting warmly at her waist, but her whole being focused on the kiss and the powerful and intense effect it created in her body. Heat flooded her core, spreading out to her limbs, squeezing the breath from her lungs as she gave herself over to the sensation. She'd never experienced a kiss like this. Chemistry, was it? Or was it that she'd never kissed a man as gorgeous and dashing as Quasar. Either way the effect was overwhelming.

She had no idea how long they kissed, but when they finally pulled apart and she opened her eyes, she found herself blinking against now-unaccustomed daylight. "Oh, dear." The words spilled out. The intense sensations pouring through her had sparked her to life in a way that seemed dangerously familiar. She hadn't felt this way since the early days of her marriage, when she was so sure that love could solve any problem, if she could just find a way.

She'd been wrong.

Quasar gave an amused frown. "'Oh, dear?' That's not the effect I intended."

She sucked in a breath, fighting the urge to fan herself. "It's just that I haven't…I'm not used to…I didn't think…" She didn't know what she was trying to say. Had she really come here to watch the birds? She was old enough to know better than to accompany a gorgeous man into the wilderness if she couldn't keep her wits about her.

Her heart fluttered in her chest, the emotions that she thought she'd abandoned back in the States scaring her. Her conviction that from now on she'd live a sensible life, free of passion and drama, had all but deserted her. Right now she wanted nothing more than to kiss Quasar again.

Which was a terrible idea. He was only here for a couple of weeks, tops. He'd made no further mention of introducing her to his family. For him this was just a diverting vacation fling. If she could enter into this with that spirit it would be fine, but she couldn't. "We should go."

* * *

Quasar felt his smile fade. Just moments ago Dani had been one with him, lost in a delicious and enthralling kiss. Now she shrank from him, her muscles stiffening. "I didn't mean to alarm you. That was a sensational kiss but I'll behave myself from now on if you prefer."

The countryside hummed with life that echoed in his body. A soft breeze tossed Dani's hair and arousal kissed her cheeks with pink. The secluded natural setting, high up above the world, was the perfect place for a little impromptu lovemaking.

But something told him that wasn't going to happen.

Dani's lips had tightened into a white line. "I need to get home."

What had changed? She'd warmed to the kiss instantly, and enjoyed it as much as he. She was giving back as much as he gave the entire time. They'd kissed for a full three or four minutes! Part of him wanted to seize her in his arms and kiss her again, so they could jump right back into that world of passion.

But he could tell that would be a terrible idea. "What's the matter?"

She shook her head, blinked. She inhaled as if to speak, then didn't.

"Is it that we don't know each other well enough?"

"Yes." She spoke fast, obviously glad of a way to respond. "But it's not just that."

"We can get to know each other slowly." He took her hand and squeezed it. It felt cold, and tightened in his grasp.

"We can't. You're leaving soon."

"Not that soon." He'd be here for at least two weeks. On the other hand, maybe that was no time at all to her. He wasn't too sure of Omani dating customs. It was probably customary for them to glance at each other across the stalls of a souk for nine months before a single word was exchanged.

But she was wearing jeans and a khaki T-shirt and looked like an American today. Even the lush green hillside with its winding, rocky trails looked like somewhere in the Ozarks. He didn't care where they were. All he knew was that he needed to keep her here. If he drove her home now he'd never see her again. "Let's climb higher so we can look down on the eagles. Maybe we'll even see their nests."

"I don't think that's a good idea." Her dark eyes wide, she looked so confused he just wanted to take her in his arms.

"Of course it is. We're grown adults and we can do anything we set our minds to." He scanned the horizon, hoping for an impressive eagle, or at least some rare sparrow to distract her with.

"I don't know what came over me. I haven't kissed anyone since…since…"

"Your marriage?"

She nodded. A furrow formed between her elegant brows. "I didn't think I'd ever want to kiss someone again."

He smiled. "And then you did."

He heard her inhale. "It was a mistake."

"I should take that as an insult." Her whole body was so tense he could tell she was deadly serious, but still he wanted to lighten the mood.

"It's not you, it's me."

"You're a lovely woman. You're single, or at least so you've told me. What's wrong with you enjoying a kiss?"

"I am single." She looked shocked that he'd called that

into question. "And believe me, I am not looking to get into a relationship ever again."

He wanted to quip that she'd found the right man for that—relationships were not his strong point—but he restrained himself. "Just because it didn't work out with one man, doesn't mean you shouldn't ever enjoy romance again."

"Yes, it does." She hugged herself as a breeze ruffled the trees. "Can we leave now?" Her eyes implored him.

"I guess we could start walking back toward the car." It was a good twenty minutes away. Hopefully he could win her around by then. "Why are you so afraid of another relationship?"

She walked ahead of him. "Being part of a couple turned me into someone else."

"How?" He walked faster to catch up with her.

"I lost myself. I became the person he shaped me into. The weak and useless person he despised." He saw her shoulders shiver.

"You didn't become that person. He just made you feel that way. Was he abusive?"

"Not physically. He never hit me." Her voice was very quiet. "He didn't do much at all. I became a victim so easily. I gave up my career, gave up my friends, stopped doing everything I enjoyed and turned into the nobody he wanted to hate." Gravel scattered at her feet as she hurried along the loose surface of the trail, over tree roots and around rocks. At this rate they'd be back at the car in less than ten minutes.

"He sounds like a jackass."

She stopped and turned around. "Yes. He was a jackass. I can see that now, but at the time I thought it was me. I lost all perspective on my own life. You can see how I don't want to get myself into a situation like that again."

"You won't. You just had the bad luck to give your heart, and your trust, to someone who didn't deserve it. Most men aren't anything like that."

"Aren't they?" A pained expression flickered across her face. "My father thinks I'm a fool."

"Then you need to get away from him, too."

"I can't. I have no job and very little money. The divorce lawyers took almost everything I had left, which wasn't much. We didn't have any assets to split and I didn't want alimony as it would have given my ex-husband a hold over me when I needed a complete break. With my—as both my father and ex-husband pointed out—useless career, I'm not likely to make money anytime soon." Tears rose in her eyes. "I guess I planned my life like a fairy tale, where I'd live my dreams surrounded by art and love. I was stupid."

She turned and started walking again, batting branches away from her face, descending the trail so fast he worried she'd slip on the loose gravel.

Quasar's chest swelled with pity. Which annoyed him. She didn't want pity. He hurried after her. "You had a job at Princeton. That's the epitome of success."

"And I gave it up because it interfered with me being home to vacuum the carpets. Obviously I didn't deserve it."

He grabbed her arm. "What kind of pity party is this? You need to turn your life around, not whine about it."

She'd stiffened at his grip, and now she tried to tug her arm away. Then a sob emerged from her throat, like the sound a wounded animal would make. "I know. I know! I hate myself."

Remorse clutched at his heart. Had he added to her sorrows by insulting her like the men who'd tried to crush her? "I didn't mean to hurt you. I'm just upset to see an intelligent and capable—and very beautiful—woman selling herself so short. You have an amazing amount of potential and you should tap into it."

Her eyes were bright with tears. "I know I do. I don't know what's wrong with me."

"Nothing's wrong with you." He'd softened his grip on her arm, but didn't let go. He couldn't shake the feeling that she'd run away if he did. "You need to believe that. And a good start would be to look around at the incredible beauty surrounding us and let yourself appreciate it for a moment."

She blinked, and a small tear rolled quietly down her cheek. She looked up and he saw the sky reflected in her gaze. A dark shape darted across her pupil: the flickering outline of a bird high above. He turned and watched a kestrel circling over them. "Careful," he whispered. "Don't show any weakness or he might come eat us."

A smile tugged at her sad mouth. "We'd be awfully big bites."

"And I'll protect you with my bare hands." He lifted the one that wasn't holding her upper arm.

"You have very capable hands for a businessman."

"I play sports."

"Oh." She glanced at his body. A flash of awareness jumped inside him. He hoped she felt it, too.

"So I'm fit enough to protect you."

"I guess that's reassuring." The smile now reached to her eyes. "And you're right. It is stunning here. I mustn't let myself get wrapped up in fear again. I'm trying to get away from that."

"Good. Because before that happened I think you were enjoying our kiss."

She looked up at the bird again. "I was." Her lip

quivered slightly. "Too much. I enjoyed kissing my ex-husband at first, too."

"I'm not him." He let go of her arm gently. She didn't run off. That was a start.

"I know you're not." She fixed her eyes on him. "It's just that I was so in love. It started with attraction and quickly spiraled into me giving him my entire life. I don't trust myself to be sensible."

"I don't trust myself to be sensible, either, very often." He was more inclined to plunge in headfirst and deal with the fallout later. "Sometimes you have to take a leap of faith. Don't lose the part of you that feels, or that cares. That's what makes us human." He couldn't stand that she thought shutting herself off from experience was the best way to protect herself from pain.

Even if she might have a point, especially where he was concerned. He didn't exactly have the best track record when it came to long-term loving relationships. "Look at the view from here." They'd reached a bend in the road and a gap in the trees revealed a clear view down to a river sparkling in a valley below them. "Isn't it amazing to see a river running here so close to the vast barren desert?"

"This whole mountain range seems to rise up out of nowhere. I guess it shows you that life can flourish in surprising places."

"And joy can flourish in unexpected places, too."

She turned sharply to look at him. "You're a flirt."

"Either that or I'm speaking the truth."

"Or both." She laughed. "I think you're very easy to take at face value."

"Good. Would you like to walk down toward the river? There's a path here—look." A narrow trail between the trees zigzagged across the hillside.

"Why not?" The sparkle was back in her eyes. "In fact, I'll lead the way." The kestrel spiraled overhead as she proceeded—gingerly—down the gravelly path toward the sparkling water in the wadi below. He enjoyed the view of her body in the fitted jeans that showed off her athletic-looking curves. The mystery of her traditional clothing had its own allure, but he preferred the what-you-see-is-what-you-get simplicity of Western clothing. Maybe mystery wasn't his thing. His hands itched to run themselves over her lithe body, but he counseled himself to take it slow. *Take your time. It will be worth it.* The last thing he wanted was to add to her burden of grief and regret. When they parted, he wanted to leave her smiling.

His own thoughts jolted him, and he almost slipped on the loose ground. Why was he thinking about their parting already? In business he always had an exit strategy in mind. Was he the same in relationships, even though he'd never admitted it to himself?

Something felt different this time, though. What were his intentions with Dani? She was quieter and gentler than the kind of women he usually dated, and that made him take their whole new relationship more seriously. He knew everything that happened between them would mean a lot to her, and that made it important to him, too. Already he felt a connection to her far deeper than such a short acquaintance would normally produce. He wanted to make her happy.

"Almost there!" She flashed him a brilliant smile that made his breath catch in his lungs. In moments like this he could see Dani shake off the shroud of fear and transform back into the vibrant young woman she was supposed to be. Her exhilaration was catching and he bounded down the last few yards like a clumsy gazelle, arriving on the pebbled shoreline at the same tizme she did.

"I wonder if the water is cold." He crouched and dipped his fingers in it. "Yes. It must be spring water."

She let her fingers play in the water. "In the old days there were underground channels that carried water hundreds of miles through the desert—all the way to the cities—without evaporating."

"Proves that in some ways our ancestors were more advanced than we are. Today that kind of pipeline is usually filled with oil."

"One day something else will replace the oil. A few centuries ago the frankincense trade was the beating heart of this area. You still see the trees dotting the landscape. Some of them are hundreds of years old, maybe even thousands. They tap them for the sap, which dries into hard chunks of frankincense. People still burn it for the aroma, though it isn't worth more than gold anymore."

"Value is always relative." Quasar splashed water on his face and neck. "Anyone in business will tell you that. Can't knock the oil, though. It made my family wealthy, though they've since branched out. Is your father in the oil industry?"

"He used to be. Right now he's employed by the latest building boom. He does pretty well but for some reason he's always complaining. I think he feels he should be a millionaire by now. He's never satisfied. He's griping about supporting me again. I wish I could find a job."

"Have you looked?"

"Here in Salalah?" She laughed. "I haven't. I've just assumed there's nothing in my field."

"Don't give up before you even try." He splashed a little water at her. She shrieked and splashed him back. Suddenly they were engaged in an all-out splash war that left them both drenched and breathless—and kissing again.

Four

Dani's clothes had almost dried by the time she unlocked the back door to the house and snuck in, hoping no one had noticed Quasar's car on their street. He could hardly drop her off at the market damp and disheveled, so she had to take the risk.

"Where have you been?" She almost jumped out of her skin at the sound of Khalid's voice.

"Why are you home from school so early?"

He stood in the hallway looking gangly and awkward in his too-small school uniform. At fifteen, he was going through a teenage growth spurt and had shot up about three inches just since she'd been home. "Our algebra teacher is having surgery. They let us go home. Why are your jeans wet at the bottom?" His eyes traveled back up to meet hers. "And why are you wearing jeans at all. I thought Dad told you to dress traditionally."

"I'm a grown-up. I can dress how I want." She attempted to sweep past him but the hallway was narrow and their elbows bumped.

"Hmm. Sounds like you were doing something you're not supposed to."

"I know. Walking around without a male relative. It's a shame you weren't here or I could have taken you with me to the dry cleaner."

"How did you get wet at the dry cleaner?" He was following her down the hallway.

"I stepped in a ditch. Someone must have just emptied water in it." The lie made her flesh creep a little. It was pathetic that she couldn't even tell her own younger brother that she'd spent the afternoon in the mountains. He'd probably be interested in hearing about the steppe eagle they saw, but she knew her father would freak out and possibly never leave her unattended again if he knew she'd been out in a car with a strange man. There was no way she could tell the truth.

Which was ridiculous. "Are you going to follow me into the shower?"

"Why are you taking a shower in the middle of the afternoon?" Her brother's question grated on her nerves. He wasn't a bad kid. She'd been trying to get to know him since she'd been back here, since the age difference between them meant they'd never been especially close. He'd only been about six when she'd gone off to the United States for college. He was very by-the-book, though. The kind of person who'd never be able to sleep at night if his homework wasn't done and his teeth not brushed. He was not someone she'd dare confide in.

"I'm hot. It's always hot here in Oman, but I guess I'm not used to it anymore."

"What's it like living in America? I bet it's pretty cool."

His wistful voice made her turn. Leaning against the wall he looked much less like an inquisitor and more like a curious fifteen-year-old. "It is pretty cool. The food takes some getting used to but there's stuff going on all day and night and more places to go than you can imagine."

"Do you think Dad would let me go there for college? He let you go."

She sighed. "I don't know." He probably wouldn't be willing to risk another of his offspring going astray. She hadn't exactly stuck with the program. "Wait until the dust has settled. I think he's still stirred up about me being back here with my life in shambles. He doesn't think America is a very good influence."

"Do you think it's a bad influence?"

She frowned. "No. It's big, though, and confusing. You have to be careful or you can just…get lost." She'd lost herself, giving her heart and soul to a man who could never be happy.

At least now she could see that the fault lay with him. It had taken some time to gain that perspective. And even now she wondered what she could have done differently. What she could do differently in the future so she didn't screw up again.

Quasar was different. Excitement flickered in her heart at the thought of him. Khalid walked back down the hall toward his own room, and she sagged with relief. She'd been afraid to even let Quasar cross her mind until her brother had taken his keen eyes off her. She worried about what he might see—a telltale sparkle in her eyes, a giveaway flush in her cheek. Even thinking about him produced a physical reaction. It was startling and disturbing.

She closed the door of her room behind her and glanced down at the wet cuffs of her jeans. She'd better hope Khalid didn't mention anything to her father. And if he did she'd better have a good story. A glance in the mirror showed that her face was tanned from their afternoon in the sun. She unwound her headscarf and let her hair fall down her back. A memory assaulted her of

Quasar's fingers raking through the long strands, of his hand pressing against the base of her skull as they kissed, so deep and long that she could barely breathe.

Quasar.

Fear mingled with the excitement flooding her veins at the memory of him. What was she doing? She'd let him kiss her. Worse yet, she'd kissed him back. Her lips buzzed at the memory. She'd told him things that she'd never told anyone else: her shame at letting her ex-husband strip away her self-confidence; her fear that she was worthless, unemployable and a disappointment to everyone.

And he was nothing but encouraging. And interested. She had to admit that that alone did a lot to boost her confidence. She smiled at her reflection in the bathroom mirror before she turned on the shower. Her ex-husband had made her feel like no man would ever want anything to do with her. Quasar had already proved him wrong.

But what did he want from her? They'd already kissed and the chemistry was palpable.

Next stop was sex. With no promises.

She'd have to be completely insane to even consider it. Every time she saw him, he occupied more of her brain space, more room in her heart. Of course it was encouraging that her heart was actually beating again, especially when he was nearby, but she didn't want it to get broken, and since she was still in a fragile state that might happen quite easily.

Quasar was a freewheeling, fun-loving guy who moved on when he got bored. Which could be next week.

The chilly water made her gasp. She needed to cool herself off. Quasar was a fun companion. An exhilarating break from routine. He was not her future, and she'd better remember that.

* * *

Sometimes when people asked too many questions it was easiest to stay silent.

Quasar's brothers and their families were all sitting around one of the hotel's private dining rooms, enjoying a lavish dinner. So far he'd managed to avoid revealing anything other than his excursion into the mountains. In the absence of further details they assumed he went alone with a sporting objective.

"Quasar all alone with the kestrels." Elan broke off a piece of bread. "You're giving me flashbacks to when you were a kid and you trained that bird to hunt for you. I think you're channeling your inner Omani again."

"Nothing wrong with that." Quasar shot his brother a smile. "And the views from the mountainside are pretty impressive."

"I am pleased that you're enjoying what Oman has to offer." Salim raised his glass. "You can help promote our country in America."

"I don't think you need any help. Isn't the hotel at capacity?" Quasar helped himself to some more rice.

"I have plans for a new hotel just north of here."

"On the beach? Or out in the desert like Saliyah?"

"Right on the shore, waves lapping at your toes. It's a property I've been saving for the right application. Celia's been dying to plan the landscape ever since I showed it to her."

Celia leaned against her husband. It was obvious she loved working with him. "It's going to be so lush. Not that you'd know it to look at the place now. I don't think there's a single plant growing there. Just some old torn fishing nets and driftwood." She rubbed her hands together with pretend glee. "But I love a challenge."

"Celia, I get that Salim keeps you busy creating oases

in the desert, but don't you sometimes want to take other jobs?" Quasar was curious about how this whole work/romance thing worked.

"I do. I was in Mexico City last month working on a corporate headquarters there."

"And the kids stayed at home with Salim?" Quasar topped off his sister-in-law's glass of lemonade.

Celia nodded. "Of course—we have plenty of help here at the hotel. And sometimes they all come with me. It's nice now that the kids are young enough that they don't have to miss school."

Elan still worked with his wife, Sara, too, though now they were business partners, not boss and assistant. Quasar couldn't imagine how you could spend all day *and* all night with someone. Didn't they ever get tired of each other? That must be what true love was like.

Most likely he wasn't capable of it. He was better suited to brief affairs. Intense journeys of exploration and enjoyment that ended while everything was still fabulous. He couldn't wait to continue his voyage into the intriguing world of Dani. Her passion was so unexpected and he suspected he'd just bumped the tip of the iceberg. It was time to take her to his private getaway in the foothills of the mountains. He'd be staying there right now if Salim hadn't convinced him to stay at the hotel to spend more time with Elan and Sara while they were visiting. He hadn't even stopped by since he'd been here.

A waiter brought a round of coffees and a plate of dates. The children were excused from the table and started to run around it like maniacs, which made everyone laugh.

Quasar had formed a plan. "Have you guys been out to my house lately? I had a decorator fix it up for me and she sent me pictures, but I haven't seen what Celia did with the landscape yet. You've all kept me so busy I haven't had a chance to visit."

"There were twelve frankincense trees on the property," said Celia. "They hadn't been tapped in years and we did it ourselves. I'm going to send you some of the finished product for Christmas."

"Does that mean I'm not invited here for Christmas?" He pretended to look sad. He did feel a little weird about the acknowledgment that he'd soon be gone. He didn't want to leave. Not without Dani.

The thought struck him like a slap. He'd been on a total of three dates with her. Something about her had captivated him. He couldn't even explain what it was. Yes, she was lovely. She was sweet. Her vulnerability coaxed out of him a nurturing side he hadn't previously realized he had.

And then there was the attraction between them. Powerful, insistent, a chemical brew that made him want to kiss her and hold her and make passionate love to her. And for that, he needed peace and privacy and a chance to get the place prepared to entertain her.

"I want to spend some time at my house tomorrow. You know, get a feel for it. There's no sense in owning a house if I never go there."

"I'm surprised you went to the mountains today and didn't even visit it."

"I planned to but didn't have time." And didn't want to scare the life out of Dani. An unplanned kiss in the wilderness was one thing. Luring her into his lair without scaring her off would take some delicacy.

"Before you become a hermit, Quasar, I want you to know that Sara and I have been hard at work searching for the perfect woman for you." Celia bit into an olive. "Do you remember her sister, Erin?"

"Of course I do." A bubbly, pretty girl with a young daughter, Erin had been at both of his brothers' weddings.

"Her latest boyfriend has turned out to be just as much of a loser as the last two." Sara took a sip of her lemonade. "So we've determined that she needs some help in the matchmaking department. We thought it might be interesting to set you guys up. It's a slight snag that she lives in Wisconsin and you live in…where do you live these days, anyway?"

"To be determined." He smiled. "I'm a free agent ready to move where the action takes me."

"Perfect. We'll have to get you guys together. There's a school break coming up in two weeks. I'll see if we can get her and Erin and her son on a flight out here."

Quasar stiffened. "I don't know, Sara. I'm not really ready for a new relationship. I want to take some time, to figure some things out." With Dani. The last thing he needed was to be set up with someone when there was no way he could be interested in her. He didn't want to hurt Erin's feelings, either. She sounded like she'd had enough of that already.

"It can't hurt to meet her, can it?"

"It might, if we meet at the wrong time and end up blowing it." He shrugged.

"I suppose you're right. It's probably better to wait until you're ready. I notice you haven't mentioned that woman you met at the bookshop. I assume she very sensibly brushed you off."

He felt a sheepish expression pass over his face. How could he keep such a big secret from his own family? All of these people wanted the best for him. Why was he so reluctant to tell them what was happening with Dani? "Actually, she was with me today."

"Ah." Salim didn't look surprised. Or pleased. Sara and Celia smiled at each other. Elan kept a poker face.

"I'll have to bring her over to meet you all soon. Her name's Dani, short for Daniyah."

"That's a pretty name. I don't think I've heard it before," said Sara.

"My lawyer was filling my ears with gossip about Daniyah Hassan the other day." Salim frowned and put his coffee cup down sharply. "It's not her, is it?"

"I don't know her last name. Isn't that funny? I'm not sure I told her mine, either."

"Well, you should have. That might have put a stop to this before it even started." Salim's expression was grim.

"Why?"

"Did she just come back from the States after a failed marriage?"

Quasar sat up. "Yes. How did you know?"

"Salalah maybe be a big city by Omani standards, but it's a small town by anyone else's. We all know each other's business."

"Isn't Mohammed Hassan the guy who sued you over that waterfront property?" Elan sipped his coffee.

"Yes. That's her father." Salim stared at Quasar. "Twelve years in the courts. That's why my lawyer's keeping tabs on the family. I don't know Daniyah personally, but her father is like a pit bull. The case still isn't resolved. Though it will be before we break ground next year. Count on it."

"Why don't you resolve it amicably?"

Salim blew out a breath. "That land is ours. Our father paid three thousand rials for it in 1976. I have the paperwork to prove it."

"Then what's the problem?"

"Old Hassan insists that his father, who sold the land,

was sick and under duress and was badgered into selling it. He claims the handshake contract is null and void, and he wants the land back." Salim crossed his arms. "Not going to happen."

"I'm guessing the land is worth a lot more now?"

Salim snorted. "Add three zeros and you're still not close. Hey, the old man needed the cash and he made a deal. I'm sure we'd all be wealthy as kings if we could renegotiate some of the bargains we made at the wrong time. Besides, it's not like he's starving. Hassan is one of the best-known engineers in the country, and he has two intelligent sons. Some people should learn to count their blessings."

"Dani's not involved in any of that. I doubt she's even aware of it. She's here to regroup after her bad marriage."

"And you're helping her out with that?" Elan crossed his arms.

"Out of the frying pan, into the fire…" Sara whispered with a wink.

"You do realize that here in Oman you basically need to marry a woman in order to kiss her." Salim leaned back in his chair, arms still crossed. "You can't carry on like you're back in L.A. Especially not with the divorced daughter of a man who's battling us in court."

Quasar regretted mentioning Dani. "We're just getting to know each other. There's nothing to even be discreet about."

"Good. Then you can break it off and no one will know." Salim arched a brow.

"Salim, you should understand from personal experience that it's not always so easy to break off an unsuitable relationship." His wife's eyes twinkled with humor. "You dumped me twice and still ended up married to me."

"That was different." His gaze, so filled with love,

made Quasar want to shake his head over the transformation of his stolid brother. "We loved each other. Quasar can hardly be in love with a woman he met two days ago."

"Three days." Quasar ate a sticky date.

"Not that you're counting." Sara winked. "Are you falling in love with her already?"

"All I know is that I enjoy her company and I want to spend more time with her." He couldn't explain the powerful feelings she brought out in him. He wanted to protect her, nurture her, make her smile. He wanted to chat with her about little things and see her eyes light up.

"I heard a rumor that her husband was abusive. She may be psychologically damaged." Salim regarded his brother coolly.

"It's true about her husband. He sounds like an ass. There's nothing wrong with Dani, though, except that she's a little wary."

"As well she might be with a lothario like you on the prowl." Elan grinned.

"She doesn't know anything about me."

Sara laughed. "Believe me, women can tell a ladies' man. You're far too good-looking for your own good, for one thing."

"But you still want to set me up with your sister?"

"I know you're a good man at heart. You just need the right woman to steady you."

"And Daniyah Hassan is not that woman," growled Salim. "A divorced woman can have a hard time finding her way in our traditional society. If word gets out that she's had an affair?" He shrugged. "Do the right thing and let her be."

"I can't believe you're worried about her reputation if her father is your sworn enemy."

"Are we the Three Musketeers? I don't have sworn enemies. I have business rivals. And her father doesn't even qualify as one. He's a mere…insect buzzing in my ear."

Quasar laughed. "Then what I do with his daughter doesn't really matter, does it?"

"The Al Mansur family has a reputation to protect."

"You work on your reputation as a ruthless and brilliant hotelier, and I'll tend to my own as an international playboy." Might as well make light of the situation. Attempts at genuine discussion were getting him nowhere. "Now, isn't it about time for me to read the kids a bedtime story?" He raised his voice so the children, who were still running around the table at full tilt, could hear him.

"Yes, Uncle Quaz! Please do!" The resulting flurry of activity was just the distraction he needed. Quasar vowed never to mention his love life to his family again. He also decided not to mention the dispute over the land to Dani. It was sure to spook her and it really had nothing to do with them. When the time was right he'd approach her father and find a solution that would make everyone happy. In the meantime, all that mattered was making Dani happy.

"It's not that far away, only thirty minutes or so. It's in the foothills."

Dani held the phone away from her ear as if removing the source of Quasar's voice would reduce its powerful effect over her. Every cell in her body yearned to say yes. She could picture the mischief sparkling in his dark blue eyes, see the arrogant and sexy cut of his cheekbones, imagine the sunlight dancing in his tousled hair.

She wanted to bury her face in his shirt and inhale the rich masculine scent of him.

"I can't."

"Of course you can." Quasar obviously wasn't the

type to take no for an answer. "I can pick you up at your house. Or any clandestine location you prefer. I'll have you back by four."

"My youngest brother was home when I arrived today. He noticed my jeans were wet. I can't take any more chances." She'd been cursing herself ever since. She was listening at the door in a panic when her father came home, wondering if Khalid would say something and expose her to inquisition-style questioning. She had no business whatsoever disappearing for another tryst with Quasar.

"Are you trying to tell me that you'll never see me again?"

Her heart seized. Is that what she meant? It seemed too awful to imagine.

"Because if that's what you think, you're dead wrong. I haven't achieved the success I've found in business by giving up easily."

She wanted to laugh. She found his persistence sexy and appealing. But then there was the other side of the story. "You freely admitted that you quickly grow bored and move on. I can't afford a casual affair. My emotions are too fragile and if that wasn't enough, my reputation is in tatters already and I can't risk it getting any worse."

"Your reputation will be as safe as the sultan's treasure. Besides, you might find the place interesting. It's an old farmhouse. I have no idea how old but possibly a thousand years or more. There are twelve frankincense trees on the property. It's a window into an earlier time."

She hesitated. History was an intoxicating drug to her. A thousand-year-old farmhouse *and* Quasar? Hard to resist. "That does sound rather intriguing."

"Ten o'clock, then. At your house?"

"No! The neighbors might see." She wanted to go,

though. How could she resist? "I'll be at the market again." The neighbors might see her there but somehow it seemed less likely. Her temperature rose at the prospect of meeting Quasar again. It was embarrassing how her resolve flew right out the window at the mere sound of his voice.

Much as it had when she'd first fallen for Gordon, against the protests of her girlfriends that he was too old for her, and too possessive. She'd been so sure of her heart. Only to watch it be trampled and left bloodless and empty.

Quasar had already hung up. Probably he was on to his next activity of the evening, barely thinking about her at all. And she faced another sleepless night of fitful dreams mixed with colorful fears and scary anticipation.

As usual the drive sped by. Quasar was so easy to talk to. He knew so many things and had been to so many places but never made her feel inadequate by comparison.

"We'll have to go to Angkor Wat together. Some of the temples seem to grow organically out of the jungle, like they really are holy and mystical creations." He talked with such conviction she could almost see them heading for the airport, ready to explore the ancient ruins of Cambodia, or Peru, or someplace she'd never even heard of.

They drove into the green-cloaked mountains, along a winding road that seemed to go on forever. High, heavy vegetation on both sides hid the outside world and made her feel as if they were driving in an alternate universe, where the dry deserts and bustle of Salalah didn't even exist.

The road finally petered out and they drove across an expanse of grass toward a building unlike any she'd seen in Oman. "Are we really in Oman?"

He laughed. "I'm pretty sure of it."

"But your house has a pitched roof. It looks like something you'd see in New Jersey!"

"It's much rainier here than the rest of the country. That's why it's green. I suppose the old farmers figured they needed a pitched roof to keep the rain out of their houses."

The stone walls had been left unplastered and had an intriguingly ancient appearance. The house was on a sloped hillside, and the frankincense trees formed an orderly rectangle on the higher side of the slope. She could easily picture sheep grazing under their scraggly branches, on the rich grassy hillside that looked like it belonged in Ireland, not Oman. "This place is so well-hidden I'm amazed you even found it."

"I spent a weekend walking in the mountains two years ago, and I stumbled across it. It was empty and falling down so I looked into the ownership. The old man who lived here had died and his family were in Muscat and didn't know what to do with the place, so I bought it from them. I love it here. It's the perfect escape from the real world."

He reached a tall wooden door, studded with nails, and punched a code into the keypad nearby. The lock clicked and he pushed the door open. "Electronic servants are so much more discreet than the human kind." He paused in the doorway and kissed her softly on the lips. Her breath hitched and a shiver of awareness passed through her.

All alone.

In private.

With a man who stirred her senses in a way she'd never dreamed possible.

The door clicked shut behind her and Quasar held her hand as they walked across a dimly lit interior room, decorated with embroidered hangings. Unlike the unadorned exterior, the inside had been renovated into a comfortable blend of minimalism and luxury. The walls were plastered smooth and the stone floor scrubbed and honed to shiny perfection. Striking pieces of contemporary furniture added pops of rich color, and eye-catching modern art ornamented the walls. The space was eclectic, warm and filled with personality and exuberance, much like its handsome owner.

Her palm warmed against his and excitement trickled along her nerves. She had a feeling he was leading her to the bedroom and the idea scared and enthralled her in equal parts.

He opened an arched door into a large, octagonal room with embroidered curtains draped over the windows, filtering the midday sun. A wide, low bed, strewn with pillows like a lovers' playground, filled the middle of the room.

She was right. And this was so wrong. But as he held her hand, she could imagine the feel of other parts of his body—his muscled chest, his sturdy thighs, his strong arms—pressed against her and the siren call of desire echoed through her.

"I'm so glad you're here with me." Quasar's soft voice was a balm to her nerves. He turned to face her and fixed those tempting blue eyes on her. An invitation to pleasure. "We won't be interrupted."

"Except by my conscience." She tried to smile.

"You're not doing anything wrong."

"Not yet. But I have a feeling I'm about to."

"It all depends on your definition of wrong. Enjoying a peaceful afternoon in the mountains with a good friend is very right, in my opinion."

"Am I really a good friend after such a short acquaintance?"

"Indubitably."

The strange word made her laugh. How did he manage to get her so relaxed? Today he wore white linen pants, rather wrinkled, and a white shirt with the collar thrown open to reveal his tanned neck. It wasn't fair for him to be so ridiculously good-looking. How could any girl resist him? They probably couldn't, so at least she wouldn't be alone in throwing caution to the wind and engaging in an illicit affair.

"I haven't had sex in…in…" She felt as if she should warn him that she wasn't some princess of delights who'd know how to acrobatically leap through twelve different positions without missing a beat. She couldn't even remember the last time she'd enjoyed sex. Her ex-husband had struggled to stay aroused enough to please her. At first she hadn't minded. Sex wasn't everything. She was a virgin when she met him so she didn't know any different and expected that things would improve with time.

Oh, how wrong she'd been.

"Good."

"Why good?"

"Because you're starting all over again, fresh and new."

"Like a virgin?" She laughed, thinking of the Madonna song.

His dark blue eyes sparkled. "Exactly."

Five

Was it possible to forget the past, or at least leave it behind? Dani reached for Quasar's shirt collar with a renewed sense of optimism. She actually wanted to undress him. She'd wondered late at night what his body looked like naked, and now was her chance to find out.

His eyes rested on her mouth as she undid the first two buttons of his shirt, her fingers trembling against his hot skin. Tanned by the sun, and hard with muscle, his chest outstripped her fantasies.

And now his hands were on the buttons of her navy blouse. His long fingers deftly pulled the tiny buttons from their holes, and she hesitated as she saw the bright white of her bra exposed. Unsure of what his eyes would do to her, she didn't dare look up at him. Instead she busied herself with the remaining buttons on his shirt, trying to keep her breathing steady as she traced the line of buttons down to the waistband of his pants.

"Stop." He took her wrist gently, which was a relief as she wasn't sure what to do when she got to his pants. "And kiss me."

Their kiss melted away the tension building inside her. Quasar's embrace wrapped her in soothing warmth. She loved that he wasn't trying to rush her into anything. Her body ached with need, and the feeling was as confusing as it was exciting. Even by American standards she hadn't known him very long. She could easily postpone this until another time—or indefinitely—and make a show of touring around the house and looking at the old books.

But she didn't want to. She wanted to see Quasar's naked body, and feel it pressed against hers. The desire alone felt so rebellious and freeing after the way she'd shut herself down—been shut down—to the point where she'd forgotten what pleasure really was. Now it lapped at her from all directions.

Her fingers found their way to the button of his pants, and undid it. He was hard, aroused as she was, and as she lowered the zipper, it thrilled her to know how much he desired her. He'd unbuttoned her blouse and now lowered his head to her bra, licking her nipples through the thin fabric.

Her hips bucked at the rich sensation pouring through her. She shoved her fingers into his silky hair and gasped at the sensation. Then he undid her bra and suckled her bare nipple until she shuddered with arousal.

She'd never wanted anyone so much. Maybe it was the years of pent-up longing, or maybe it was just Quasar, but she wanted to make love to him so badly she could taste it. "You have a gorgeous body." She'd lowered his pants down his legs to discover that they were as muscled and powerful as his torso.

"Me? You're the one with the gorgeous body." He'd already removed her shirt, and now he unzipped her pants and eased them down over her thighs. "Look at that hourglass waist. And a man could lose himself in between these luscious thighs." He crouched and buried his head between them, suddenly flicking his tongue in her most private place and making her gasp. When he licked again, she let out a tiny high-pitched noise that might have been embarrassing if she were with anyone but Quasar.

"Oh, my." She didn't know what else to say. She clung to his shoulders, enjoying the tensed muscle under her fingertips. Arousal rushed through her, leaving her breathless. Every inch of her was alive with sensation. Quasar's tongue flicked back and forth, sending little shudders along her legs.

"Lie on the bed," he commanded softly.

She obeyed, her body almost limp with desire. She eased herself up onto the soft covers and let herself relax. Quasar bent over her, kissing her body, stroking her, and licking her most sensitive flesh until she could barely stand it. "I want to feel you inside me," she whispered. She couldn't remember ever wanting anything more intensely.

"It would be my pleasure." His low murmur was the sexiest thing she'd ever heard. She could hardly believe it was her lying here on this bed, writhing with delight. Even being naked with Quasar felt completely natural. The warm air kissed her skin and the soft, diffused light was gentle on her dilated pupils.

He rolled on a condom, then eased his strong body on top of hers and entered her very gently. He looked right into her eyes at the moment of penetration in a way that said, *I'm here with you right now and nothing else matters.*

Arms wrapped around his back, she welcomed him into her and gave herself over to the strange and wonderful sensations flooding her body. He filled her, making her gasp and moan with pleasure. It seemed impossible that just a few days ago she'd been alone, sure she'd never feel a man's arms around her again. In fact she hadn't wanted a man anywhere near her. She'd grown afraid of masculine energy and its demands. She preferred the safe solitude of her bedroom and the comfort of quiet loneliness.

Meeting Quasar had changed everything. He had been so sweet to her from the moment they met. Kind and encouraging, nonjudgmental, supportive… He was like a fantasy come to life—in the form of a breathtaking man with boundless confidence and the world at his feet. And now here he was, making love to her with all the power and passion he possessed and driving her into a realm of intense bliss.

"Oh, Dani." His voice rasped in her neck. "You're doing something to me. I'm losing control, I…I…" He climaxed with a dramatic shudder and, breathing hard, clung to her. "I don't know what happened." His arms wrapped around her, holding her close. "I meant to last longer but…" His words trailed off into her hair.

"It was perfect," she murmured, wanting to reassure him. And it was. She'd climaxed so powerfully that her muscles must have gripped him and driven him over the edge, whether he was ready or not. The thought made her want to laugh. That she had so much control over such a powerful and commanding man was funny and made her feel sexy. "I've never had an orgasm like that in my life," she admitted.

"Good." He heaved a sigh. "Me neither." He laughed, letting his head fall next to hers. "I don't know what you're doing to me, Dani, but everything's different. It's just so…different."

She laughed.

"See, you're making me inarticulate with passion. Usually I'm a quick-witted charmer, but around you I just…" He pressed his cheek to hers for a second, and she enjoyed the masculine roughness of his skin. He kissed her firmly, then softly, then firmly again on the mouth. He was still inside her, and she felt him throb, and her own sex respond. It made her smile. She couldn't remember that ever happening before. Her body was having a conversation with his body, an intimate conversation that had nothing to do with their brains, or her fears, or anything other than the sensations and emotions they created together.

"I'm not too articulate at the best of times, but I have no words to describe how I'm feeling, either." She stroked his hair and nuzzled his cheek. His skin smelled fabulous, rich and musky, with a hint of fragrance like some ancient incense. "Except that I feel very, very good."

"I'm so glad. You deserve to feel wonderful. Your lover should make you feel cherished and special and beautiful, and it pains me that you've ever felt otherwise."

"You're making up for it right now." She smiled, and kissed his nose.

"Good. From the sounds of it I have a lot of making up to do, but I'm up to the task."

"I have no doubt about that."

"I promise you I'm a skilled lover, when I'm not overcome by unexpected and intense feelings." His dark gaze met hers, and she enjoyed the sparkle in his eyes.

"I'm glad I was able to overwhelm you. I'd think an experienced lover could get jaded and bored easily." Pride tickled her that Quasar was so excited that he literally couldn't contain himself. Who'd have thought that little Dani—as her ex had derisively referred to her—could have that effect on a man?

Quasar eased out of her and she watched as he walked to the adjoining bathroom. His body was magnificent, sculpted like a bronze statue, and he strode with the lithe confidence that characterized everything he did.

Part of her couldn't believe her luck to be here with him right now.

The rest of her wondered how she'd hold up when it was all over.

When he was wrapped around her it was easy to forget that her time with Quasar was limited. Everything felt so effortless and perfect she was tempted to assume it would go on forever.

But there was no forever. Everything in human existence had its time limits and her time with Quasar would be a few more weeks at the most. She tried to tell herself it was freeing to know that the relationship had a sell-by date and she didn't have to worry about it turning sour like her marriage. Still, she'd miss him.

"Why so serious?" His silhouette filled the bathroom door. She hadn't noticed him watching her.

"I know I should make the most of our time together, but I can't help thinking about the future."

He frowned, and she regretted her frank confession. "It's better to live in the moment."

She felt his comment like a stab to the chest. He was right, of course. All the philosophers pretty much agreed on that point. Happiness was in the present moment. Everything else was just an idea or a memory. "I'm going to miss you when you're gone." Her whispered words hung in the air.

It was pretty amazing that she was still confident enough to admit her true feelings. But that was the cool thing about Quasar. She knew she could say anything and nothing bad would happen. Her ex had been so touchy that she had to carefully vet every phrase that came out of her mouth to make sure it wouldn't get under his thin skin and make him fly off the handle.

"I'm going to miss you, too. I'll miss you tonight when

you're alone in your bed in your father's house, and I'm alone in my bed in my brother's grand hotel. It does seem a crime that we can't be together." His eyes brightened. "Why don't you come stay with me?"

She stared. To him it was a simple practical consideration—*I won't miss you if we're together*—and he'd come up with a practical solution.

That wasn't practical at all.

At least not if she wanted to preserve what little was left of her reputation. Ending a bad marriage was embarrassing but not utterly fatal to her future prospects. Openly engaging in a sexual affair with a man she wasn't married to, in full view of his family and the whole world, would be almost up there with hanging a red light outside her window.

"I mean it. My brothers are both married to Americans. They're not old-fashioned. They'll understand."

"I can't. I intend to live in Salalah for the time being so I have to abide by the customs or I'll quickly become a pariah. I swear some people already cross the road when they see me coming. I've committed a multitude of sins in their eyes by running off to America and marrying Mr. Wrong."

Quasar sighed. "I suppose you're right. Still, wouldn't it be wonderful for us to spend the whole night together?"

Or the rest of our lives? The stray thought popped into her mind and she quickly banished it.

He stroked her cheek softly. "Are you sure you can't think of an excuse to stay over?"

His persistence amused her. "I'm not that clever."

"Usually I am, but you've disarmed me so much that I'm not on top of my game." His mischievous gaze made her smile. He leaned forward and murmured in her ear.

"So I think we'd better make love again and see if I can get my sanity back."

Desire tickled her insides as his low voice stirred her senses. "That sounds like a good idea."

"At least I still have some good ideas left." He trailed a finger along her torso, tracing a line between her breasts, and down over her belly, which twitched as he passed it. "And some condoms."

She giggled. The prospect of feeling him inside her again was ridiculously exciting. She felt like a kid about to unwrap a bar of her favorite candy. If someone had told her a week ago that she'd be gazing at the naked thighs of the most gorgeous man she'd ever met, she would have laughed in that person's face. If someone had told her she'd ever even be excited by the prospect of sex with a man again she'd have expressed some doubt. Just a few days had transformed her from a wary, shy recluse into a sensual woman ready to risk her heart for a few brief moments of pleasure.

Her heart could handle it. It must be steel-plated by now after all she'd been through in the last few years. As long as the affair was secret and no one else knew about it, she could deal with her private pain when it was over.

Quasar lay on the bed next to her, and she ran her hand over the hard muscle of his thigh, letting desire rise inside her like flood water. Already he was erect again, ready for her. She watched his taut belly contract as she lowered her lips and licked him. He uttered a low groan when she took him in her mouth, and again she loved the power she had over him—power she intended to use only for pleasure, never to hurt him. She enjoyed feeling him grow harder still as she pleasured him with her tongue, then she eased herself up and trailed kisses over his flat stomach with its sprinkling of rough, dark hair.

Her ex had a hard time maintaining an erection and coaxing it back from the dead had become a tiresome chore she dreaded. This was clearly not an issue with Quasar. After he'd rolled on the condom, she climbed over him, and eased herself down on top of him slowly, reveling in each delicious moment of sensation as he filled her.

Her ex hadn't liked her to go on top. He liked to be in command of everything and probably didn't want her to think her pleasure was hers for the taking. Quasar's broad smile and blissfully closed eyes showed her that she was welcome to enjoy him however she liked. She smiled as she moved her hips, and rich, intense waves of pleasure started to roll inside her. "This feels so good," she murmured. It was wonderful to choose the rhythm, and control the motion, with their mutual pleasure as her only goal.

"It feels even better for me," he rasped. His fingers stroked her skin, gently rubbing her nipples and driving her even wilder with excitement.

Already her breathing came in ragged gasps and it was hard to form thoughts. Something inside her took over and she found herself quickening the movements as powerful feelings washed through her. When he climaxed with her, moving inside her as her muscles gripped him, the intensity of the sensations made her cry out. She felt so close to him at that moment, with nothing between them, no worries or anxieties or hang-ups, just a shared burst of joy bringing them together.

How could this be wrong if it felt so good and didn't hurt anybody? She collapsed gently on top of him and his strong arms closed around her back, holding her close. His chest rose and fell beneath her and emotion welled inside her. In his embrace she felt so supported and cared for and cherished, just as he'd said she should. Which was silly, since they really didn't even know each other that well. There was a connection between them that neither of them could fully understand or articulate, but it was there all the same.

She wrapped her arms around him and buried her face in his neck. She wished she could stay here forever, pampered by his affection and his simple enjoyment of her company.

"That was something else, Dani." His gruff voice and the gentle way he stroked her hair almost undid her. Their bodies seemed to fit so perfectly together, still throbbing and pulsing with enjoyment even as they lay quietly in each other's arms.

"You're something else." She wasn't telling him anything he didn't already know, and that was okay. She didn't even mind being one in a long stream of eager women. Why not? It was the most pleasure she'd ever experienced during sex; she'd probably never know anything like it again. "And I'm very glad you interrupted my reading that day."

"Me, too. It pains me to say this but it's almost time for you to leave."

"Already? I feel like we just got here." A glance at her watch revealed that he was right. How had three hours flown by so fast? And how sweet of him to keep an eye on the time for her when he could have ignored it in the pursuit of his own pleasure. "I really wish I could stay, but we both know I can't."

"Can you come back tomorrow?"

She smiled, her face still pressed to his neck. "I'd love to."

The next day they could hardly wait until the drive was over before they peeled off each other's clothes and made steamy, passionate love again. The attraction between them was so intense it threatened to singe their flesh. Dani had never known such powerful desire. It undid her inhibitions and let her revel in pure enjoyment for its own sake. Afterward, they wrapped themselves in luxurious silk robes from the bedroom closet, and unpacked a lunch Quasar had brought from the hotel. They were in a room that had been remodeled into an open kitchen and living-room area. The ancient pale stone walls contrasted with the light-filled modern spaces, and stained-glass lanterns sprinkled glittering jewels of color over the walls and ceiling.

"Goodness, look at this salad. It must have twenty different things in it." There were lush slices of fruit, nuts, fresh greens—everything looked as if it had been picked that morning.

"Salim scours the world for the most creative chefs and makes them an offer they can't refuse."

"It must take some convincing to get them to come to Salalah. I bet most of them have never heard of it."

"Money talks." Quasar grinned and spooned helpings of the salad he'd brought into beautifully painted earthenware bowls.

"Not to everyone."

"Sooner or later, most people will listen to it. That's my experience, anyway."

"That's a very mercenary view of the world." She poured them both a glass of fresh limeade with fragrant mint leaves.

"True. What do you think motivates people?" His gaze contained a challenge. She resolved to rise to it.

"I think most people want to be happy. I know I do."

"To a certain extent I agree." He stretched out on one of the sofas, dish of salad balanced on his knee. "The problem is that no one really knows what makes them happy. They rarely even know when they are happy. They just notice when they're not."

"And they decide that a few more zeros on the end of their bank account balance will make them feel better?"

"Pretty much." He winked.

It was hard to counter, since she wasn't motivated by money at all. She'd been lucky enough never to have to worry about where her next meal was coming from. Family loyalty might come with obligations, but they were amply paid back by the security her family offered when she needed it most.

On the other hand, was she happy?

She looked at the gorgeous man seated on the sofa next to her, contentedly munching on the exotic salad. Right now, the answer was unequivocally yes. She was happy. She knew it wouldn't last forever, or even for much longer, but right now she was in bliss.

"I'd like to meet your father."

"What?" She almost dropped her fork.

"It's not right for us to keep meeting in secret. We're in Oman and we should abide by Omani custom."

She swallowed hard. "I don't think that's a good idea."

"Why not?"

He won't like you. And with good reason, since you've tempted me into an illicit affair. "You're only here for a short time. There's no point."

"Of course there is. We don't have to tell him we're having sex, but at the very least he should know we're friends."

"But we're not friends." *We're a lot more than that. Or much less.* She wasn't quite sure. Her stomach had shriveled into a tiny knot. Her feelings of blissful happiness were evaporating into the air-conditioned atmosphere as she faced the true nature of their relationship head-on.

Quasar still looked relaxed and at ease, sipping his limeade. "Don't worry, I'll charm him."

"He's not really susceptible to charm. He's an engineer. He's all about structure and substance." *He'll want to know when the wedding is.* She couldn't say that. She'd rather die. A pleasure-seeking international playboy like Quasar would not be marrying her in this lifetime. Even in the throes of passion she wasn't delusional enough to think that.

"Trust me."

She shook her head. "Trust *me*. It's not a good idea. Besides, I don't like being told what to do. That's what my ex-husband specialized in, remember?" She was proud of herself for speaking her thoughts. She didn't need a man to run her life and tell her what was appropriate. Not that she was pleased with herself for sneaking about, but under the circumstances it seemed like the only approach that protected both her feelings and her reputation. Quasar cared about her feelings because he wanted to please her, and her father cared about her reputation as a matter of family honor, but neither of them really had much reason to worry about the big picture.

"I don't want to tell you what to do, but I don't like this sneaking around. It doesn't sit well with me. We have nothing to be ashamed of."

"You just admitted there was no reason to tell him that we had sex." She noticed how he called it having sex, not making love. "So it's not like you wouldn't be hiding something anyway. It will be easier for me if he never knows about us."

"I've spoiled your appetite for this delicious food." He looked ruefully at the fork now sitting idle on her plate.

"I'm sorry. I'll drop the subject. If you want me to be your secret lover I'll try to go along with it."

She managed a smile. "I bet this isn't your first secret affair."

"I cannot tell a lie. I'm no stranger to subterfuge. I think I'm getting too old for it, though. I'd rather have everything aboveboard."

"Sometimes that's just not possible. Besides, you're thirty-one. That's not old."

"I'm a mature man and you're a mature women and we should be able to enjoy each other's company openly."

"In America, maybe, but not in Oman." Things would be so different if they were in New Jersey, or California. On the other hand, if they were, Quasar would probably be spending the afternoon with a glamorous starlet or a sexy businesswoman, and would never have noticed her. She didn't exactly have men pursuing her everywhere. Her cousin said it was because she gave off energy that said, *Stay away!* Her ex had been persistent enough to break through her reserve. Then he'd been persistent enough to steamroll right over her and empty her life of anything but him. She didn't know how to have a normal relationship. Her affair with Quasar was anything but normal but maybe it could be if the circumstances were different.

If they weren't in Oman.

If Quasar were an ordinary man.

If she were an optimistic, confident woman who still believed in love and happily-ever-afters.

But none of those things were true so she had to make the best of where they were right now. She picked up her fork and tried for an encouraging smile. "I appreciate you wanting to meet my father. It really is sweet of you. It just isn't a good idea."

"I'll bow to your superior wisdom on the topic. You've lived in Oman a lot longer than I have." He didn't look mad, or even put out. Probably it didn't matter much to him either way and he'd just made the suggestion to please her. Which was sweet.

She forked some salad into her mouth and let the sweetness of orange and mango spread over her tongue. She needed to live in the moment. To be happy while the opportunity presented itself.

Which shouldn't be hard given the circumstances. Diffuse sunlight poured through the lattice screens on the arched windows, pooling in luxurious patterns on the marble floor. Quasar's slate-blue eyes sparkled with the passion and excitement that she'd put there. In bed he'd been making love to her with a look of rapture on his face. Who wouldn't be happy in her place?

It wasn't as if she were falling in love with him. Now that would be stupid. She wasn't stupid. They'd enjoy each other's company, then they'd go their separate ways. There was no danger of getting in over her head. In the meantime she just needed to keep her head, and protect her heart.

"I can see you're not hungry, beautiful." Quasar put down his plate and knelt at her feet. He kissed her fingertips, then her lips, and desire flared through her, banishing her doubts and worries. "Shall we go back to the bedroom?"

She placed her plate on an inlaid wood table. Feeling was so much easier than thinking. Right now all she wanted to do was press her naked body against Quasar's and lose herself in his touch. "Absolutely."

Six

"I'm telling you, leave well enough alone. Her father hates our whole family." Elan reined in his horse, who was blowing hard. They'd trailered two horses, borrowed from a close friend, and headed out to the mountains to let off some steam. They were up on a high slope with a view of Salalah partially visible through the trees.

Quasar leaned back in his saddle on his gray mare, who was puffing and blowing from the effort of the ascent up the mountain. "But I can reason with him, make a deal that will win him over. I'm famous for negotiating my way out of tough situations."

"Or into them. Are you going to marry her?" His brother's intense gaze slammed right into him.

"I just met her."

"See? You're just experimenting. Playing around. Seeing what will happen. And I think we both know, based on your history of relationships, what will happen."

Quasar frowned. "You think I'll grow bored with her."

"I don't know her. How could I predict that?" Elan leaned forward to flick a fly off the neck of his sturdy chestnut gelding.

"I want to bring her over so you can all meet her."

"That will tell her that you're serious."

"I am serious!"

"Not by Omani standards. Serious means marriage. Don't lead her on until you know where you're going."

Squinting into the late afternoon sun, they guided their sweating horses down a winding trail on a wooded slope. "How do I know where I'm going if I don't at least get started in the right direction. Did you know right away that you would marry Sara?"

Elan laughed. "Hell, no! I was determined to have nothing to do with her. She was my employee, for crying out loud."

Elan had not only had an affair with his secretary, but he'd also accidentally got her pregnant. "But you ended up in the right place, married to the woman you love."

"Yeah." Elan took a gulp from his canteen. "I learned to stop being the boss and trying to run the show, and let Sara be my partner. So if Dani doesn't want you to meet her father, then don't."

"I see your point."

"You can't charm your way into every situation. Or out of it. Old man Hassan hates our family with a passion that could last for generations. If you can manage not to fall in love with his daughter you'd probably be doing both of you a favor." Elan's familiar piercing stare caught him off guard again. "You're not in love with her already, are you?"

"Me?" Why couldn't he stop thinking about her? Wanting to be with her? Wanting to tell everyone about her? Was that love?

Probably not. Nevertheless, it was likely some possessive male thing that would still get him into trouble.

"Because if you're in love with her then it's a different story."

Their horses were happy to reach level ground. Elan launched into a spirited description of the newest Arab mare on his ranch back in Nevada. "Women aren't like mares, little brother." Elan pulled up his horse and stared at him again. "They don't like being told what to do. They need to make up their own minds."

"I suppose you're right." Of course he didn't love Dani. He barely knew her. They had great chemistry, no doubt. Unbelievable sex, hell yes. Interesting conversation, for sure. Enjoyable companionship, yes indeed. But love? He didn't even know what that was.

"Then don't approach her father. If you do, he'll think you're serious. And if you don't love her, you're not serious. Shall we gallop on this flat land?"

"Sure." His mind whirred with confusion as he urged his horse faster, until the gray mane was flying in his face. Why were matters of the heart so much more complicated than corporate affairs? Since coming to Oman he'd already come up with three viable new business plans, each of which excited him equally. On the other hand, there was only one woman on his mind.

"Race you there!" Elan called back, pointing to a lone frankincense tree in the desert.

Whipped on by his own competitive instincts, Quasar charged forward until they were neck and neck, their powerful horses speeding across the desert, hooves tapping out a quiet drumbeat on the sandy soil. Pursuing Dani was all wrong. He didn't want to hurt her again after what she'd suffered in her marriage.

When his horse passed Elan's, Quasar let out a yell into the desert air. A whoop of triumph that also contained a howl of frustration at the situation he found himself in with Dani. The sex they shared was insane. He could talk to her about anything. He craved her company when he wasn't with her. And everyone, including her, thought he should stay away from her.

So why did he want to ignore them all and take matters into his own hands?

"Good news, my darling." Dani's father arrived home that evening in an uncharacteristically festive mood. She didn't remember ever hearing him call her *darling* before. It struck a note of alarm in her heart.

"What, Dad?" She took his briefcase and put it in its place under the hall table.

"Samir Al Kabisi came to my office today." He was beaming. Dani froze. This was the man who'd told her he was still potent so her needs would not go unmet. "He made a generous offer for your hand in marriage and you'll be happy to hear that I accepted."

"What?" She knew the custom of *mahr*, in which the husband offered a certain sum of money to his bride. It was a tenet of Islam intended to protect women by making sure they had money of their own in case they needed it. But these days it was customary for the man to make his offer of marriage to the woman herself, not her father, wasn't it? And how could her father possibly accept without asking her? Her heart pounded and her breathing grew unsteady. "I'm not marrying him."

"Don't be foolish, Dani." Her father's cheerful expression had barely altered. "It's an excellent offer and he's a good man. He owns his own firm and could comfortably retire tomorrow if he wanted. He's the chief supplier of nuts and rivets in the gulf region."

"But I'm not in love with him." Her voice was shaky. She knew her father couldn't make her marry this man, but her refusal was bound to cause a rift between them.

"Love grows. It's a silly modern fashion to try to fall in love before you're committed."

"I'll never love him. He's too old. I'd make him unhappy as well as myself."

Her father's expression darkened. "Daniyah, I've been very indulgent with you since your unfortunate return home. You tried to do everything your own way once, and the results were disastrous."

She didn't deny it.

"Now it's time for you to listen to the wisdom of your father and an older generation, when life was simpler and people were happier."

She couldn't argue and say that her parents' marriage wasn't happy. She suspected it wasn't but since her mother wasn't alive to agree with her, she could only speculate. "I'm not opposed to marrying again, but it needs to be someone I can grow to have feelings for."

"Samir is a kind man. He hosts a party at the orphanage every year during the *Eid* holiday."

"I'm sure he's lovely, but those aren't the kinds of feelings I'm talking about. We're both adults here. If I'm to share a bed with my husband I must have some attraction to him."

Her unruly brain conjured an image of Quasar next to her in bed, languid, his tanned, muscled body against the white sheets, eyes shining in semidarkness.

"Daniyah, I'm shocked at you. Discretion is an essential quality in a woman."

"I have to speak the truth. I've survived one bad marriage and I'm not willing to take a chance on another. You'll have to tell Mr. Al Kabisi that I refused his kind offer, or I'll go tell him myself."

Her father clucked his tongue, his good humor utterly gone. "A father does not expect to endure the burden of his daughter returning home in middle age."

Stung by humiliation, Dani drew herself up. "I'm hardly middle-aged. I'll find a job."

"As an art historian?" He snorted. "You should have studied something sensible, as I always encouraged you to. You could have been an engineer, or a chemist, or even an architect, but no, you had to study something foolish and whimsical with no career prospects, almost as if you intended only to be a rich man's wife."

Tears stung her eyes. "Art is my passion."

"Fishing was my passion, when I was a child. I did not, however, choose to become a fisherman. If I were still inclined to pursue it, I'd fish simply as a hobby."

She had to admit his words made sense. She'd been so blinded by the cheerful attitude that everyone should follow their bliss, which had prevailed at the small New Jersey university she'd attended. "You're right. But I'll find something. I'll work in a shop."

He looked doubtful. "At least take the night and think it over. You'll be very comfortable with Samir. He has a spacious house only a few streets away and he drives a Mercedes."

"I won't change my mind," she whispered. "I have a headache. I'm going to go lie down." She'd skip dinner and help herself to something later when everyone else had gone to bed. She couldn't face sitting around with three male Hassans looking skeptically at her every move.

Not for the first time she reflected that maybe she should have stayed in New Jersey, where at least she wouldn't have elderly suitors shoved down her throat. But how? New Jersey was very expensive. She had no job and no place to live, and she could hardly return to live with her aunt, who had four daughters and now considered her to be a bad influence. Her self-esteem had been shattered by her ex-husband and she no longer believed herself capable of supporting herself and living independently. At the time she'd seen no other option than to run home with her tail between her legs.

Now that she'd had the time and distance to regain some perspective, she could see that coming home actually left her in a worse position. Her employment prospects were dimmer than ever, and she had another domineering male to answer to.

In her bedroom she lay on her soft bed and gazed up at the high ceiling with its ornately carved wood beams. This house she'd grown up in was grand by Omani standards. She'd always been well provided for and treated like a princess, at least by her indulgent and warm mother. She'd seen little of the world outside the filigree wooden shutters and had imagined it to be a brilliant and exciting place similar to the one she saw on American television shows. In college she often felt like the star of an upbeat sitcom where anything was possible. When her future husband, Gordon, had arrived on the scene, she'd assumed she was the heroine of a romance being swept off her feet by his insistent pursuit.

As her marriage progressed she'd realized she might be starring in a future episode of *Law & Order* instead. As her husband's psychological abuse ratcheted up slowly into verbal abuse, and he began to pound his fists on the table or the wall, she knew she'd be next to feel his wrath and she'd finally come to her senses.

Hot tears leaked from her eyes as she reflected on all the foolish dreams she'd had. And now Quasar had come into her life as if to mock her with the kind of romance and passion she couldn't really hope to enjoy, at least not for more than a few stolen sessions.

Noise from outside her room made her jerk her head

up from the pillow. She heard raised male voices, and one in particular made her breath catch in her throat.

She could almost swear that was Quasar's voice.

Dani climbed off the bed and hurried to her bedroom door. The house was one story, centered around a hallway, and if she opened her door the men would likely see her. The voices seemed to be coming from the direction of the front door.

"I know exactly who you are," her father was shouting. "Your whole family has played a part in the plot to deprive my heirs of their birthright."

What? Dani pressed her ear to the door. Now she was desperate to hear the other voice. It couldn't be Quasar, could it?

"Mr. Hassan, I come with nothing but the utmost respect for you. You may not be aware that I have lived in the States for many years and have little to no involvement in my family's affairs. I certainly have played no part in the lawsuit between our families."

Dani's chest rose and fell rapidly. It did sound like Quasar. But it couldn't be, because she'd explicitly told him not to come here. And if it was Quasar, they'd be talking about her. And they weren't. She had no idea what they were talking about.

She frowned and turned back toward her bed. Obviously she was losing her mind if she thought some random man who came to the door must be her lover. When she wasn't with him, thoughts of him haunted her day and night. His image always seemed to hover at the edges of her consciousness, taunting her until she could see him again. He'd talked her into letting him pick her up at the house tomorrow. He'd convinced her that repeatedly meeting out in public was getting too risky and it was wise to mix things up a little, so she'd given him her address.

Her chest—and other parts of her—tingled with excitement at the prospect of seeing him again and spending another languid afternoon in their remote and luxurious love nest.

But what on earth was going on in the foyer?

"I curse the name of Al Mansur and I will never let one of those sons of dogs anywhere near my daughter!"

Dani froze; the word *daughter* struck fear into her heart.

"I'm not here as a representative of my family or anyone else. I come simply as a man of honor seeking your approval to meet and talk with her."

Now she was sure that the voice was Quasar's.

She crept back to the door, blood pounding in her head, and pressed her ear to it. Oh, how she wished there was a keyhole to peer through!

"My daughter is spoken for. A man has just today asked for her hand in marriage, and I have accepted his offer."

"Surely Dani must have a say in the matter." Quasar sounded shocked. As well he might. She hadn't mentioned her father's plans to him. "She's an adult woman, not a young girl who doesn't know her own mind."

"She's made up her own mind in the past and it proved to be a bad idea. She understands that I have only her best interests at heart."

Dani could stand it no longer. She tugged open her bedroom door and stepped out into the hallway. "What are you doing here?" she heard herself ask Quasar. She stood, staring at him. He looked oddly regal in traditional Omani attire—it was the first time she'd seen him in it—but she was furious with him for going against her wishes.

"You are a respectable Omani woman, and I am a respectable Omani man, and it is customary for me to meet your father and ask permission to court you."

"Permission is *not* granted!" growled Dani's father. "And I do not give you permission to place your accursed feet in my house. What do you have to say for yourself, Daniyah? Have you encouraged the attentions of this reprobate?"

She swallowed. "I…"

"She has done nothing whatsoever to encourage my attentions. I simply noticed that we both share a taste for books, and a brief discussion suggested that we have some interests in common. I would like to get to know your daughter better." Quasar turned his gaze to Dani, and those deep blue eyes seemed to hold her in a trance.

"I didn't ask you." Her father scowled at Quasar. Then he turned his attention to her. "Daniyah, have you spoken with this man?" She'd never seen her father so angry. His eyebrows stood on end like little furry animals, and his lips had grown white.

"Yes, Father. I have spoken with him." If he had any idea what else she'd done with him, he'd probably have a heart attack on the spot. She couldn't think of anything to say that wouldn't either incriminate her or enmesh her in a lie she'd later regret.

"Your daughter's conduct has been unimpeachable."

Dani stood rooted to the spot. That was a very subjective view of her conduct, which by any traditional standards was shocking in the extreme.

"If you don't leave my house right now, I'll call the police."

"Sir, let me beseech you. I'm happy to simply exchange a few words with your daughter here in your house, under your watchful eye."

Quasar seemed totally unfazed by her father's apoplectic rage. If anything she thought she saw a twinkle of humor in his eye. Which, under the circumstances, really ticked her off. He'd taken no personal risk coming here. If her father hated him, who cared? He was going back to the States and would soon forget the whole affair.

She, on the other hand, would have to live with the repercussions of this ill-starred visit for the rest of her life. "You really should leave." She found herself speaking coolly, looking directly at Quasar. How could he have totally disregarded her wishes? She'd told him not to come. Who did he think he was?

"If Daniyah wishes for me to leave, I shall leave." He swept a bow in her direction. The chivalrous gesture would have excited her if she weren't almost as angry as her father. Quasar nodded to the older man and apologized for alarming him, muttered a traditional goodbye and left, striding confidently in his long white dishdasha.

Dani wanted to sag with relief as he disappeared out of sight, leaving the front door open to the gathering dusk. Instead, her instincts told her to turn and run.

Her father calmly and quietly closed the door. "What is the meaning of this, Daniyah? You are not in Hackysack."

"It's Hackensack."

"I don't care what it's called. You are in Salalah now. You can't strike up a conversation with any Tom, Dick or Harry who happens to stroll past you in a shop! You must have encouraged him to give him the confidence to come knock on my front door. Do you have any idea who this man is?"

She shook her head mutely. She didn't, really. It was hard to believe she'd never even asked his last name. It hadn't been relevant. And maybe she hadn't wanted to know. It would have made their relationship seem more real, and then it would hurt more when it turned out to be a dreamlike interlude, as she knew it ultimately would.

"Quasar Al Mansur is the youngest son of Hakim Al Mansur."

The name sounded vaguely familiar. She'd never paid much attention to local society gossip but she suspected he was some kind of oil-rich sheikh.

"Hakim is mercifully no longer on this earth, but his sons continue to refuse to recognize our family's ownership of the old Fabriz property. They tricked my father into selling it for a few thousand rials when it was simply a mediocre fishing spot. Now it's worth millions as prime waterfront investment property, and they're maintaining that the pathetic deal he was forced into is valid."

"If it was his father's doing, Quasar probably wasn't involved at all." After she'd spoken she realized she sounded as if she were defending him. Her best course was to pretend she barely even recognized him.

"I've had a lawsuit pending against the Al Mansur family in one form or another since the eighties. I haven't won yet, but I haven't lost, either. Salim Al Mansur has been itching to build one of his accursed hotels on that property for years, but he hasn't been able to because the title is clouded by my lawsuit." A look of satisfaction crossed his face for a moment. "It's only a matter of time until my rights are legally recognized and the property is returned to our family. Your brothers deserve to reap the riches that can be sown there, not those grabbing Al Mansurs, who already have more land and money than they know what to do with."

Dani blinked. She'd known the family was wealthy

and powerful, but it was just her luck that the first man she fell for would be her father's sworn enemy.

She wanted to go back, lie on her bed and continue crying. But that wouldn't solve any problems. "I won't see Quasar behind your back." The resolution was easy to make. He'd deliberately ignored her plea that he not come here. He obviously didn't care about what she thought and had run roughshod over her own thoughts and wishes just like her ex-husband would have. She was done with him.

"But I won't marry Samir Al Kabisi, either." She screwed up her courage. "I'm not ready for marriage again, Father. It's too soon. I'm sure he's a nice man but I'm also sure that any attempt to match me with him would lead to disaster for myself, disappointment for him and further damage to my reputation. I'm sure you don't want that."

"Indeed I do not." His eyebrows were starting to subside a little and color was returning to his pursed lips. He sighed. "Things were so much easier in the old days when a girl listened to her parents."

The next morning Dani woke with a heavy weight in her chest. It was all over. She'd known her affair with Quasar couldn't last forever, but she'd secretly hoped for a couple more weeks of romantic bliss. Last night had put an end to that. She'd promised her father she wouldn't see him in secret, and she meant it.

She'd done an internet search on Quasar's name and the results had been alarming. There were more stories about his love life than his many business triumphs. While she looked at the seemingly endless stream of photos of him, accompanied by an assortment of gorgeous women at movie openings, nightclubs and celebrity parties, it sank in that she really was just another notch on his bedpost.

The day stretched ahead of her like the barren desert. She could do some shopping for food, but even the cleaning was taken care of by a kind older woman who'd been alarmed by Dani's offers of help, probably fearing she'd soon be out of a job.

She resolved to stay under the covers in her bed and read until she regained her equilibrium. After about five minutes, though, she grew restless. She was not going to lie around and wait for life to happen to her. She needed to make it happen, and right now that meant finding a job. Maybe one of her brothers' schools could use an administrator? She decided to visit their offices, and showered and dressed conservatively in a dark green ensemble with that intention. She was arranging her hair when she heard a knock on the door.

She glanced at her watch. It was ten o'clock. The time she'd previously arranged to meet Quasar.

She stood staring at her shocked reflection in the mirror. Could he really have just shown up as if nothing happened?

Another knock, this time more insistent, stirred her to action. If it were Quasar, she had to get him off her doorstep before one of the neighbors saw him. She hurried down the hallway and peered through the peephole. The sight of Quasar's handsome face made her breath catch, as it always did. She braced herself against the effect he had on her and opened the door. "Come in, quick."

Already she was breaking the promise to her father, but it was to prevent further gossip, so hopefully he'd approve.

Quasar stepped over the threshold, his face more serious than usual. "Good morning, Dani."

He bent down to kiss her, but she ducked back, heart thudding. "You shouldn't be here. I told you not to come."

Quasar had the decency to look a little wistful. "I was hoping to make a good impression. I thought if I could talk to your father, he'd see what a nice fellow I am, despite any rumors to the contrary."

She wanted to laugh. Or cry. "And now you can see how wrong you were. I told you not to come and you totally ignored me. Did you know he's suing your brother over some piece of land?"

He shrugged. "I did know. I was hoping to find a resolution to that problem as well."

She fought the urge to growl. "You're so arrogant! Charm can't fix everything. In fact it probably can't fix anything at all, ever. I can't believe you knew our families were at odds and you didn't even tell me. I was so clueless and naive I never thought it was important to know your last name. Even I've heard of the Al Mansurs."

"So if I'd told you my name from the get-go you would have run a mile in the opposite direction?"

"Absolutely."

"Then discretion was the better part of valor."

"Hardly. Now my father is furious and doesn't trust me. If he had any idea what we've already done together he might throw me out on the street. I probably deserve it."

By Omani standards she'd been the worst kind of loose woman. At least she wasn't sleeping with a married man, but beyond that the situation had no redeeming features. "You need to leave."

"I came to see your father because I really care about you, Dani." Quasar's gaze fixed on her with the intensity of a laser. "I didn't want to sneak around like we're having some meaningless dalliance. My brothers warned

me that if I came to see him he'd think I meant business."
He frowned. "And I do."

Dani's heart was beating so fast she couldn't think,
let alone speak. Did he mean that he wanted to marry
her? No, he hadn't said that. She cursed herself for even
being foolish enough to think it. "You have to go. The
neighbors might have seen you arrive."

"I'm not leaving unless you come with me." He seized
her hands and held them. Her hands were so cold inside
his. "Don't tell me you don't have feelings for me."

Nameless emotion flared in her chest. "I have feelings all right. I'm angry with you. You deliberately did
something I told you not to."

"Come with me and let's talk about it. At least allow
me that much." His slate-blue gaze implored her.

Common sense warred with much stronger feelings
as he held her hands and kept his eyes locked on hers.
Could she really just make him leave without an expla-
nation? Her heart said no. "Okay, we'll just talk. Nothing
more." If his car was parked outside, she wanted it gone.
"Let me get my shoes."

Once outside the house, she glanced furtively in both
directions and dived for his silver Mercedes. She prayed
no one had seen it. At least it was such a popular car here
in her affluent neighborhood that it didn't say a whole
lot about its owner. She climbed into the passenger seat
and donned a pair of dark glasses that were sitting on the
shelf above the glove compartment. "Quick, drive away
before someone sees us."

"You're making me feel like I'm in a spy movie."

"You'll be in a very different kind of movie if my father discovers that you came here again."

An infuriating smile played around the edges of Quasar's mouth. "Why? What would he do to me?"

"He did threaten to call the police. He'd do it, too. His cousin Ahmed is the chief of police."

"Ouch. I'd better keep my head down, then."

She sank back into her seat as they pulled out on to the main road. She hadn't seen anyone she recognized. On the other hand, she was now heading who-knew-where with Quasar, when she'd sworn to stay away from him.

Adrenaline fired through her. "I can't believe you totally ignored what I told you. You decided to take charge of my life, regardless of what I think. Just like my ex." She stared right at him as she said the last part, daring him to argue with her.

He turned to look at her, and she was gratified to see contrition in his eyes. "I didn't think of it like that. I'm sorry."

"You should be. The last thing I need is another man telling me what to do. Or even worse, not telling me! It was not a pleasant surprise to hear your voice in my hallway." It felt good to voice her feelings. She'd been afraid to do that for so long.

"I thought that if I talked your father around, you'd be happy about it."

"Your confidence is both awe-inspiring and infuriating. Who knows my father better, you or me?"

He shrugged and looked sheepish. "You. I confess I'm not used to waiting around. I prefer to get up and make things happen."

"Typical male."

"I suppose so. Do you think you can forgive me?" Already she saw the twinkle of familiar humor creeping back into his annoyingly seductive gaze.

"No way." She focused her gaze on the windshield. It was dangerous looking at Quasar. He was far too handsome for his own good, or anyone else's.

"What am I going to do with you?"

She decided that his seductive tone was only going to fuel her anger. "Say goodbye to me for good, and drop me home." She snuck a sideways glance at him, just long enough to see if she was immune to his charms.

The answer was no.

He turned to face her again, a mysterious glow in his eyes. "I have a much better idea. Come meet my family."

Seven

Dani's response was immediate and came straight from her gut. "That's a terrible idea."

"I disagree. You'll like them."

"If you meeting my family was an unmitigated disaster, what makes you think me meeting your family will go better?"

"I'm willing to take a chance." Quasar had already steered the car in the direction of the ocean.

"You're obviously more of a risk taker than me. But that's hardly a surprise since you like extreme sports and I like reorganizing my bookshelves. We have almost nothing in common."

"Nonsense. We have something very important."

"Chemistry?"

"Something bigger than that. Call it a life force. Something you can't ignore."

"Says who?" Dani noticed with alarm that they were now driving past the palaces of Salalah's wealthiest citizens.

"Me. And I'm right more often than you'd think."

"Not about love. I did a Google search of your name last night, now that I finally know it." She watched for his reaction and wasn't surprised when a muscle twitched in his cheek. She didn't say more. She was curious to see what his response would be.

"What did you learn about me?"

"That you're known as a fickle maverick entrepreneur in the business world, and that you've dated a large number of beautiful women."

"I can't deny either accusation. I have been fortunate to enjoy the company of some wonderful women." His smile was barely apologetic. "But none of them outshone you."

Pride and embarrassment threatened to heat into a blush. What a flatterer! She shouldn't take his words to heart. "Did you march over and meet their fathers?"

"No. That should prove to you that what I feel for you is different."

They drove through a tall archway with scrolled gates that opened before them. Panic flashed over her. "Wait. You can't just drive in here. I haven't agreed yet."

"Too late. We're here." Salim drove calmly along an avenue of date palms.

"A man who tells me what to do is my worst nightmare." She wiped her now-sweaty palms on her forest-green dress. At least she'd gotten dressed up today. Was he really going to drag her in to meet all his *über*-successful relatives?

"A woman I'm crazy about who tells me never to see her again is my worst nightmare. So at least we're even." He smiled. "Relax. Don't worry about impressing them." He must have seen her fiddling with her scarf. "They're very nice, really."

"Like you?"

"I actually think I'm probably nicer than both of my brothers. They're a little scary, at least when there's business involved. Both of my sisters-in-law are lovely, though. They'll put you at ease."

"Even though they have no idea I'm coming! What if they're busy?"

"They're not. I know they're planning to spend the day relaxing on the beach with the kids. Everyone's on vacation right now."

"I'm not exactly dressed for the beach."

"Don't worry about that. They'll have everything you need in the hotel shop. And don't try to pretend you wouldn't feel comfortable in a swimsuit. I've seen your gorgeous body with my own eyes." The wolfish look he gave her should have sent her fury into overdrive, but instead it had the far more irritating effect of making her aroused.

"What if I don't want to meet your family?" His arrogance was almost unbelievable. This whole escapade was further proof that he was all wrong for her.

Quasar steered the car into a large circular driveway with a spectacular fountain in the middle. She'd heard about this hotel before. It was insanely expensive and very exclusive. It looked like a sultan's palace. Further proof that Quasar Al Mansur was out of her league in every possible way.

As well as being a total jerk.

He parked the car and took her hands in his. "Dani Hassan, I like you very much. Getting to know you better is important to me, and I want you to get to know me better as well. If you then decide that you hate me, I can handle it." That familiar sparkle of amusement lit his eyes. His hands warmed hers and softened the frigid wall of reserve she'd tried to build around herself. "But please do me the honor of meeting my family. It would mean a lot to me."

Her heart swelled when he spoke with such apparent sincerity. Of course this was probably how he'd behaved with all those beautiful women in the gossip column photos. But who was she to think she could resist him any more than they could? If an A-list actress hadn't been able to say no to Quasar, she didn't stand a chance. "Okay."

Before she could gather her thoughts, a bellhop—wearing a uniform the exact same green as her own clothes—opened her door, and she stepped out into the bright sunlight. Quasar immediately rounded the car and threaded his arm though hers, as if hoping to forestall her escape. She glanced around nervously. What if the family felt much more strongly about the land dispute than Quasar, and considered her their enemy?

Even if they were friendly, what if one of her father's associates were here? Or a neighbor? Or almost any ordinary citizen of Salalah who might gossip at the souk about who they saw on Quasar Al Mansur's arm?

She tried to calm herself with the thought that she'd been in the United States since she was a teen so people weren't likely to recognize her. And most of the guests looked foreign, judging from their scanty attire.

"They're probably still having breakfast. That's where they were headed when I left them less than half an hour ago. Things tend to move very slowly when the whole family is gathered together." He led the way into a grand lobby with tall arches and rich mosaics on the walls, and through it to a series of sunlit dining rooms. In the farthest one, a veranda with a view over the beach, she saw a group of people laughing around a large round table. The two blonde women must be his American sisters-in-law. They both glowed with good cheer and the effects of the Omani sunshine. Four children, ranging in age from two to about six, wriggled in seats next to them, finishing the remains of pastries and scrambled eggs. Two tall and handsome men sipped their coffee and looked with calm indulgence over their rather messy offspring.

"I'm so glad you're all gathered in one place." Quasar's deep voice immediately commanded the attention of the group. "I have someone very important for you to meet."

Dani blanched as he said her name, wondering if they'd react with hostility or disdain. Their warm smiles and greetings soon put her at ease, though, as Quasar made his way around the table introducing each one. The taller blonde was Celia, the landscape designer, who was married to his oldest brother, Salim. Her husband looked more than a little forbidding in his dark pinstriped suit, but he made her promise to make herself at home at the hotel. She was relieved that he didn't even mention the lawsuit.

Muscular Elan looked much more casual in jeans and a white T-shirt. He laughed when Quasar apologized for dragging her here, and consoled Dani that the Al Mansur men do need some retraining at first. Elan's wife, Sara, was sweet and welcoming and said that she was just getting to know the vast hotel complex herself and still got lost here sometimes.

A waiter brought two new seats and baskets of fresh pastries and fruit, as well as another pot of coffee, and to her surprise she soon found herself and Quasar making easy conversation with them about life in America versus life in Oman. She relaxed a bit as it became clear they did not consider her to be their enemy simply because of her father's lawsuit.

"Quasar pretends he lives in the States but lately he spends as much time here as he does there," teased Salim. "He even has a house out in the desert because staying at my hotels isn't homey enough for him."

Dani froze. They obviously had no idea she'd seen his house in the desert and tested the firmness of the mattress.

"I like to enjoy the best of both worlds. I come here to relax and unwind and step back to a simpler time. Now if only I could find someone trustworthy enough to look after a falcon for me when I'm in the States, my life would be complete."

"You should have seen him hunting with the falcon he had as a kid." Elan leaned forward and looked warmly at Dani. "He caught and trained it himself and he would spend all day out there in the middle of nowhere in pursuit of some imaginary quarry."

"You'd be surprised how many rabbits we brought home for Mom's cooking pot. All it takes is patience."

"Most people don't have that kind of patience. To look at your life now, I wouldn't have guessed you did, either," said Salim. "I can't believe you just sold another promising business that you could have taken to the next level."

"It was time to move on." Quasar sipped a glass of berry-colored juice.

"See? You're always looking for the next big thing."

Quasar frowned. "Maybe that's what I've been doing wrong lately. Too much rushing, not enough waiting." He looked at Dani and the expression in his eyes made her breath catch. "It's possible that I got off track and now I'm finding my way back. I can be as patient, steady and persistent as the Al Hajar Mountains themselves when I need to be."

She blinked and swallowed, then looked away. Did his whole family know about their relationship? She couldn't believe he was speaking so intimately in front of them. She felt as if he were trying to convince her he could be the kind of reliable, steady man she could count on. On the other hand, maybe he was just talking about falconry.

"Lately Salim's taken up sailing," said Celia. "He said it's both humbling and awe-inspiring learning to work with such powerful forces as the wind and the currents."

"Yes." Salim raised a brow. "I don't think I would have been ready for it if Celia and Kira hadn't already quietly demonstrated to me that the world doesn't revolve around me, I'm simply part of a much bigger picture."

Sarah laughed. "I think the Al Mansur men attract energy like a vortex. You all have to learn to use it wisely."

"And perhaps that is best accomplished with the help of a good woman," said Quasar softly.

Everyone looked surprised, perhaps that he was speaking so frankly in front of Dani. She wasn't sure he'd even mentioned her to them before. She pretended to be busy tugging apart a croissant. Did Quasar really have such strong feelings for her? It was a little intimidating. She hadn't let herself dare to imagine that he might feel anything beyond attraction and lust. They hadn't known each other long enough.

And her father hated the whole Al Mansur family with a fiery passion.

"Dani, is your father Mohammed Hassan?"

She felt her eyes widen at Salim's question. Apparently the time for niceties had passed and he was going to bring up the lawsuit. "Yes."

"Our father paid for that land fair and square," Salim continued. "There's no written contract because…"

"Because my grandfather couldn't read or write." She'd heard the sob stories about an illiterate fisherman being cheated out of his legacy. And his brilliant, self-educated son—her father—devoting his life to getting it back.

"Exactly. But that doesn't invalidate the deal. A hand-shake was as good as an iron-clad legal document back then. Still is, to men of honor."

She bristled. Was he trying to say her father wasn't a man of honor? He wasn't the warmest person in the world, but he'd worked hard to provide an excellent life for his family. Right now she felt guilty at not always appreciating the sacrifices that must have involved. "I confess I don't know much about the matter except that my father feels very strongly about it."

She glanced at Quasar, wondering what he was think-ing. It was quite rude of his brother to bring the matter up. Was he hoping she could convince her father to drop the suit?

"Hardly anyone in Oman could read or write before 1970." Quasar shrugged. "We were still living in much the same way we had in the Middle Ages. Sultan Qa-boos started a slow revolution that has created an edu-cated populace and modern infrastructure, but kept the heart of our traditions. I'm pretty sure he would think a handshake contract is binding."

"Why don't you ask him next time you're riding one of his spectacular cavalry horses?" Elan sipped his cof-fee. "Quasar became buddies with him a few years ago when he sold him a little gray mare he'd trained for tent-pegging. They go riding together around his estate."

"I doubt he'd be interested in a piece of empty coast-line. He likes to talk about emerging technologies. I swear I thought he was going to buy that networking software company I sold three years ago."

Dani was speechless. Quasar rode with Sultan Qa-boos? She'd seen the sultan in parades and he always seemed like a figure from an ancient myth, not someone you could have a ride and a chat with. More proof that Quasar lived in an elevated realm far above hers.

"Of course the original contract is binding," murmured Salim. "Money changed hands. That in itself is a contract. And although it appears a small sum now it was quite reasonable at the time. It's provoking that this lawsuit is clouding the title when I'm now ready to develop the property."

Dani frowned. Her father's lawsuit was actually preventing the Al Mansurs from going ahead with their plans? A cold shiver ran through her. Was it possible that Quasar had actually brought her here with the ulterior motive of putting pressure on her to get her father to abandon his suit?

Maybe all along he knew who she was and he'd approached her with the explicit aim of winning over her father. That would explain why he came to the house to press his claim on her, even when she'd asked him not to. Her croissant stuck in her throat and she tried hard not to search their faces. Were they all in on some conspiracy against her family?

"Why can't you pay Mr. Hassan enough money to buy his good graces?" Quasar suggested brightly, as if the idea had just occurred to him.

"Don't think I haven't thought of it." Salim sighed. "But I find in business that when you offer an olive branch like that it can be turned against you as proof that your original claim on the property wasn't valid. It's usually better to hold one's course until the storm is over."

Celia caught Dani's eye and shrugged. She looked embarrassed. At least someone was. She couldn't believe they were discussing this right in front of her as if she weren't there. Unless it was part of some plot. Why hadn't Quasar intervened to stop the conversation?

"Are you hoping I can convince him to drop the suit?" She finally spoke up. It was either that or run from the room, and since she'd resolved to take control of her life, speaking up was better.

"Of course not." Quasar looked shocked. "I'm sorry it's even come up. Salim, you're making my guest uncomfortable. I brought her here to meet you all and get to know you and you're stirring up some family feud that has nothing to do with her. I'm so sorry." He looked so genuinely contrite that she almost forgot her ideas that this visit was part of a scheme to end the land dispute.

Almost.

"That's okay. As I said, it has nothing to do with me. I wish my father would drop his lawsuit but I really don't have any influence over him in the matter."

The children had grown restless during the boring adult discussion and were now chasing each other around the table. "I think it's time to hit the beach," said Sara. "I'll grab the towels and sunblock if someone else could bring the sand toys."

"I'm on it," said Elan.

"I'll herd the children," said Salim, with an indulgent smile at them. And just like that they were all headed for the beach. Dani wasn't sure whether she liked being bundled so easily into the family group. Her nerves jumped when Quasar touched her a couple of times as they walked along the elegant allée of date palms that led to the beach. Part of her was excited and flattered to be here, and the rest was terrified that she was in way over her head.

They spent about two hours building a magnificent kneeling camel out of sand, kept damp by an elaborate network of canals hand-dug by Elan and his son, Ben.

When the camel was done, it was solid enough for the children to climb carefully onto its back and "ride."

No further mention was made of her father and his land claim. In fact the conversation centered around education and the dilemmas that the Al Mansur parents were facing regarding the benefits of homeschooling their children so they could travel freely, versus letting them enjoy the social environment of a real school. Both families had decided to travel and homeschool while the children were younger, then worry about where to settle so the kids could enjoy more stable social lives once they were in their teens.

It was refreshing to hear people who thought nothing of living part of their lives in the States and part in Oman. When she'd moved to New Jersey for college her Omani friends had been appalled and swore that she'd never come back. You'd have thought she'd decided to colonize deep space. When she met her husband and settled there, with her father's stern disapproval, she did indeed wonder if she'd ever see Oman and her brothers again. It had taken a lot of courage and humility to come back, and at the time, her departure from the States had seemed final and permanent.

Now she wondered if in fact she could make a life that involved both places. Her expertise seemed to lend itself to that, if she could just find the right niche. She felt invigorated and excited about her future by the time Quasar pointed out that it was time for her to go home.

She was forced to admit, on the drive back, that Quasar's family was both warm and welcoming and that she'd actually enjoyed herself. She'd almost forgotten her fears that they'd brought her there to convince her to win her father over.

Until Quasar brought up the subject. "How much do

you think your father would take to drop his claim on the land?"

"Are you serious?" Her worst fears flared up again.

"Why not? It would solve a lot of problems. He might even start to like me if I can resolve this issue that's been nagging at him for decades."

She snuck a sideways glance at him. Was he interested in her because she could help him solve the land problem, or was he interested in the land problem because it could help him win her?

It was too confusing for her to tackle. "I don't think he'd take money at this point. I think he wants the land back."

"What would he do with it?"

"Sell it on the open market, I suppose. But there's no way to know what it's truly worth until he does that. He says the location is so prime there would be multiple offers for it."

"Salalah has a lot of empty coastline."

Suspicion flickered inside her. "Not in the middle of town."

"You'd be surprised. It may not be worth as much as he thinks."

Her throat tightened. "I have no idea what it's worth and I don't want to get involved." She wanted to get home and away from Quasar before he charmed her into anything else.

"What about one million dollars? American money."

Now she was really getting upset. "I don't know. It's not my land. You'd have to ask him." If this were the real reason for his visit last night it would explain why he didn't care if she wanted him to meet her father or not.

"He says he won't negotiate with an Al Mansur."

"Then you have your answer." She checked her watch.

It was nearly three-thirty and to be safe she needed to be home by four. Her youngest brother often got home from school around that time. Luckily they were already in her neighborhood.

Quasar sighed. "I wish I could convince my brother to just give him the land. Now that you've met Salim you can see that Salalah would have to freeze over before that happened."

She softened. "If Salalah froze over the hotels might not be so popular. Unless he opens a ski resort in the mountains."

Quasar laughed. "I suspect he'd like the way you think." He pulled on to her street and drove up to the front of her house. Then he glanced both ways and drove around to the back entrance. "I can't stand to leave you. I want to spend more time with you."

I want to make love to you. She read the words in his gaze and they echoed in her heart.

Was this part of his charm? A slick gloss over an ulterior motive? Or was Quasar really as smitten with her as she was with him?

"Can I come in, just for a moment?" His soft words scandalized her.

"You've got to be kidding. I promised my father I wouldn't see you again. You've already made me a liar and now you want to trespass in his house?"

"I've been accused of having a different set of morals than most people."

"I don't think that's a good thing." She gathered her bag off the floor. "I have to go."

"Kiss me."

His gaze, hooded, dark and filled with passion, stole her breath and every last ounce of her common sense. Suddenly her lips were on his, kissing him with tenderness. His arms wrapped around her in the cramped space of the car, and his exhilarating male scent filled her senses. The effect he had on her was shocking. Once minute she was normal and sensible, the next...

"I'm desperate to make love to you." He gestured to the house with his head.

"No way. You're crazy."

"Kiss me again, then." He covered her mouth with his before she had a chance to refuse. His hands on her body stirred passion that grew into an ache. He pulled back just enough to look into her eyes. "You know you want to."

"I do, but..." The prospect of making love with Quasar in her own bedroom was terrifying and electrifying at the same time. Her whole body burned to feel his pressed against it. "We'll have to be really quick." Heart pounding, she extricated herself from his embrace and climbed out of the car. She couldn't believe she was about to do this, but apparently that wasn't enough to stop her. It was a crazy foolish risk but somehow that felt right. She'd been tiptoeing quietly through life, putting her own needs and desires last for far too long. Following her instincts felt daring and liberating.

The back door had a key code and she unlocked it and ushered him down the dim hallway past the empty servants' bedrooms. "In here." She ducked into her bedroom and pulled him with her, locking the door behind her. Her familiar bedroom, with its calming lilac walls and floral-patterned bedcover, looked utterly different dominated by the tall and commanding presence of Quasar.

Within seconds they were grabbing at each other's clothes and shucking them off to reveal bare, anxious skin. Dani clutched at him, pressing her chest to his, reveling in the closeness that banished all her doubts about his intentions.

He wanted her. Nothing else.

Quasar kissed her face, her neck, her hands, with worshipful passion. He kissed her thighs, her knees and her ankles. Then, easing her back onto the bed, he licked her sex until she gasped with pleasure.

For an instant she was distracted by the framed picture of her high school class photo, then by the stuffed bear her friend Nala had given her. Things that reminded her there was a real world out there beyond Quasar's intense embrace. Then she forgot again and folded herself into him, watching with joy and impatience as he donned a condom. Welcoming him into her and moving with him on her familiar bedspread, letting sensation and emotion wash over her like a tidal wave she couldn't fight but could only hope to flow with.

They climaxed in a rush of almost unbearable tension and release that made her cry out so loud that Quasar clapped his hand over her mouth and startled her. Eyes gleaming with arousal and amusement, he urged her to be quiet and not give them away.

She watched her own chest rising and falling as if she'd run a marathon. "What have you done to me?"

"Awakened you." He kissed her cheek softly, his eyes closing for just that instant. "You were like the sleeping beauty, sleepwalking through life. Now you're living in the moment."

"Living like a crazy person." The clock on her wall said 3:45 p.m. "My brother Khalid could be home any minute."

"You can tell him I'm the mailman."

She smiled. "He'll know you're not. The real one gives him gum sometimes."

He put on a mock serious expression and pretended to check his pockets even though he was naked. "I don't have gum." He let go of a wistful sigh and stroked a finger along her body. "You're beautiful, and sensual, and affectionate, and I can't get enough of you."

"Sorry to disappoint you yet again but you need to leave *right now*." Half-playful and half-serious, she pushed him off her and reached for her clothes. It was hard to tug them on. Her whole body was trembling with excitement and something akin to shock.

"What if I won't go?" Sprawled across her single bed, he knitted his hands behind his head and pretended to ease farther onto the mattress. "Then what will you do?"

"That's not funny. I hate bossy men, remember?"

He smiled and rolled up and onto his feet. "I'm not really bossy. I'm just…" He seemed to think about it for a moment.

"You're just trouble." She picked up his pants off the floor and threw them at him. "Get dressed and get out of here." Even while she pretended to scold him, excitement at their escapade rippled through her. They were both healthy, consenting adults. Why couldn't they enjoy each other's company?

Quasar pulled his pants on far more slowly than she liked. She tried to bundle his arms into his shirt to hurry him up, but he ended up grabbing her around the waist and kissing her until she wondered if they'd need a second condom.

Then she heard something and froze. Footsteps in the hallway.

Eight

"It must be Khalid." Her heart was jumping around in her chest.

"Why don't you introduce me?"

Dani motioned for Quasar to be silent. "He probably saw you here last night. He certainly heard you. There's no way we can pretend you're just a friend, even if it wasn't totally inappropriate for me to have a male friend come visit me here alone. We have to get you out of here without him seeing you."

"I'll climb out the window." He looked amused by the idea.

"You can't. It has a grating over it. It's locked from the outside and I don't know where the key is."

"That sounds very dangerous in case of a fire."

She motioned again for him to be quiet. Now was not the time to worry about fire safety. He shrugged his shirt on, quickly buttoned it and examined the window. "Will he come in?" He gestured toward the hallway.

"No. But he might wonder why I haven't come out to say hello. I'll have to pretend I was napping and didn't hear him come in." It was hard to speak quietly enough that the sound wouldn't travel into the hallway. "Maybe you should hide behind the door. I'll go distract him with something in the kitchen, and you can dash out the hallway past the servants' quarters."

"It's lucky you don't have any servants." He tucked in his shirt. "I'll sneak out like an experienced diamond thief."

Dani's heart was in her throat as she opened the door with Quasar hidden behind it. If her brother saw her he'd rat her out for sure. He wasn't mean but he was a Goody Two-shoes. She'd been one at his age, too.

"Khalid? Is that you? I fell asleep!" She hurried down the hallway toward the living room. Her brother often threw his bag down in there and lay on the sofa before he started his homework. "Could you help me get the lid off the new olive jar? I've been trying all afternoon." She had to lure him into the kitchen. It was the only room where you couldn't see into the central hallway. She prayed that Quasar would be patient enough to wait.

"Dani! I'm resting. Give me a minute."

"Oh, come on. I'll make your favorite snack. Anything you want."

"Well, in that case…" He eased off the sofa. She held her breath as he glanced in her direction. The hallway was clearly visible behind her. Then he turned toward the kitchen and she followed him, hoping there was an unopened olive jar somewhere.

"What did I do with it?" She made a big show of clattering around in the pantry, trying to make as much noise as possible while straining her ears to hear if Quasar had made his escape. "Oh, here it is. I don't know why it's so stuck. I even put it under hot water. I couldn't get it open." She glanced over Khalid's shoulder as she handed him the jar.

He opened it without a moment's hesitation. At that exact moment the back door clicked shut.

"Did you hear that?" Khalid wheeled around. "It sounded like the door."

She shrugged. "I didn't hear a thing. Thanks so much for opening this. What would you like to eat? I could make *halwa* if you like. Aunt Nadia gave me a new recipe."

"I swear I just heard a car engine start back there. I'm going to check."

She grabbed his sleeve. "Wait, there's a bottle of oil I couldn't open, either. Just do that before you go. And do you want me to make the *halwa?*"

"Sure, *halwa* sounds good. But it takes a long time and I'm pretty starving so I'm going to grab something else while I'm here." He dove into a packet of crackers. By the time she found a bottle of oil and looked impressed while he opened it, she'd quizzed him about his homework and he seemed to have forgotten about the door and the car and was telling her to make sure the *halwa* was sweet enough.

As soon as he returned to the living room she locked the back door and hurried to her bedroom to rearrange the disordered bed. The condom wrapper lay on the floor like a pointing finger of accusation and she quickly crumpled it up and shoved it down into the toe of a boot she didn't wear often.

She sagged onto her bed as waves of guilt and relief crashed over her. Was she completely out of her mind? She'd let Quasar make love to her in her bedroom, only hours after promising her father she wouldn't see him anymore.

He had a frightening amount of power over her. The worst part was that she was so willing to do all the inappropriate things he suggested. Her ex-husband had talked her into doing all kinds of things she didn't want to because he'd pout and whine and make such a fuss if she didn't. It was impossible to imagine Quasar doing that. He'd just smile and shrug and seduce her until she wanted to do it even more than he did.

Her body still tingled and pulsed with the sensations Quasar had created inside her. A quick examination of her face in the mirror showed her lips were pink from kissing and her hair messy. Lucky thing her brother wasn't too observant, and she'd mentioned waking up from a nap. Still, she'd taken a huge risk that her father would discover her affair. He would go ballistic if he found out what she'd been doing. He might even throw her out of the house.

Quasar was making her careless. Reckless. Which was all well and good while he was there and she was having the time of her life, but she'd have to live with herself and what little reputation she had left when he was gone.

Her phone pinged. And she grabbed it out of her bag.

Made it.

She smiled. He hadn't sent her a text before. Of course this was just one more piece of incriminating evidence, like the condom wrapper. She resisted the urge to respond and quickly deleted it. And now she had to go make *halwa* from scratch. At least creating the sticky dessert would keep her busy!

Another ping. I miss you.

Her heart seized. Did he really? She supposed he must or he wouldn't be texting her. She couldn't resist typing back, I miss you, too. She turned off the volume on her phone so her brother wouldn't get curious.

Being apart like this is foolish.

She frowned. What we're doing is foolish.

No, it isn't. I need you.

The tiny words on her screen made her breath catch and she told herself to get a grip. It wasn't as if he'd told her he loved her. Not that she'd even believe it if he did.

I need you, too. She wanted to type the words. But she didn't. It was much safer to keep her feelings secret.

You have an alarming effect on me. That was less incriminating and no less true.

He responded immediately. The effect is mutual. I can't stop thinking about you.

She glanced over her shoulder. You really shouldn't text me. Someone might see it.

Come to the hotel tomorrow. Ten-thirty?

She paused, and inhaled very slowly. I can't. I have to go see about a job. She'd gotten sidetracked today, but establishing her independence would be the first step to securing her own future. If she made money she could rent her own apartment and see—within reason—whomever she chose. Even Quasar, if he still wanted to.

After that, then. How about two?

Could she? Of course she wanted to. The prospect of going all day without seeing his mischievous smile was grim. But she had to be sensible. I won't have time.

I can't go a whole day without seeing you.

She couldn't help smiling. Sure you can. You've been through many days in life without seeing me. She headed out of her bedroom, and down the hallway to the kitchen.

That was before I met you. Now everything's different.

She bit her lip. She could almost swear he was sincere. Then she remembered the twinkle of humor that always hovered in his slate blue eyes. Was Quasar ever serious about anything?

If you don't agree, I'll come back right now.

Dani frowned. Part of her knew that the humor was still there and he was just teasing. The other part, that had been bullied and ordered around for nearly five years, coiled up ready to strike. That's not funny.

"Who are you texting?"

Her brother's voice made Dani look up with a start. She hadn't noticed him there in the doorway. "A friend from the States." Not exactly a lie. Not exactly the truth, either.

"Cool. I could end up at school there, too. Dad thinks I might be able to get into MIT."

"Really?" She was surprised their father would even consider it after the way she'd gone off track. "That's great. It's one of the best schools in the world."

"I know. They have an aerospace engineering program."

"I didn't know you were interested in rockets." She could feel her phone vibrating, but she resisted the urge to look at it.

"I'm more interested in satellites. You'd be surprised how important they are these days. All our information is bouncing around in space. It's the new frontier in information technology." He glanced at her phone, which was vibrating. "I think you're getting another message."

"Oh." She pretended to glance casually at it.

I'm still crazy about you even though you're ignoring me.

"I can't get used to people being able to contact me wherever I go. I'm not sure I'm ready for all these new frontiers."

"I think it's awesome. Tell your friend I said hi." He smiled and headed off to do his homework. Dani blinked and felt another vibration.

I'm on your doorstep.

Her blood ran cold. He wouldn't, would he? Did he have that little respect for her wishes and her reputation? Her heart squeezed.

Just kidding.

She narrowed her eyes. *You're really starting to tick me off.*

You still miss me, though, don't you?

She hesitated for a minute, and pursed her lips. *Yes. But don't come here. We need somewhere very discreet to meet. I'll text you in the morning.* What if someone saw this conversation on her phone? She deleted the thread, shoved the phone into the pocket of her pants and pulled out the sugar and cardamom and rosewater to start her preparations for *halwa.*

* * *

The next morning Dani donned a conservative blue ensemble and headed for the university campus. She'd printed her resumé and intended to drop in on the administrative offices and ask about available openings. Her interview with the human resources coordinator was humbling. Although she had a Ph.D. and had published several papers, didn't know any of the new database software and had no office or management experience. She'd been so successful, or lucky, at finding great mentors and work in her field that she'd never had to develop the peripheral "fall-back" skills most people her age had.

Although they had three administrative openings, none of them was "quite right for her." Friends in college had teased her that a degree in art history was preparation for would-you-like-fries-with-that? jobs. Maybe they were right.

Keeping her chin in the air, she went to the history department, thinking that perhaps she could get her foot in the door by volunteering her time here. The older building was barely air-conditioned and looked neglected and run-down compared to the rest of the state-of-the-art campus. Apparently the school put more stock in the future than in rehashing the past—and could she really blame them for that? When it came to the modern world, her academic expertise was of limited use.

An older man in a rumpled dishdasha was pinning something to the cluttered notice board inside the door when she entered. "Excuse me, does this department have an art collection?"

He looked up slowly. "Art collection?" He snorted. "I think not. There used to be a collection of swords but I think it was sold off when the roof needed fixing." He looked her up and down with some distaste and she got the distinct feeling he didn't approve of her. "This department focuses exclusively on military history. Unless you're looking for a collection of ancient battle maps, you're in the wrong place."

"Oh. Thank you." Deflated by his hostile gaze, she turned and left. As far as she'd been able to discover, the other universities nearby were entirely science- and technology-oriented.

She stopped into a boutique selling pretty traditional dresses and asked about a job there. The owner, a rather glamorous middle-aged woman, was kind, but said that currently she didn't need help.

As she walked through an unfamiliar souk in a neighborhood more than twenty minutes from her own, she realized it was a good place to meet Quasar. He answered his phone immediately and eagerly agreed to meet her there right away.

Feeling better already, and trying to hide her smile, she walked among the stalls, and tasted a sugary date. She even bought a bag of almonds so she wouldn't look as if she were only there to meet her lover. She still couldn't believe they'd made love in her bedroom. It was so wrong, and yet so exciting and exhilarating.

"Hello, gorgeous." Quasar's low voice in her ear made her spin around and her grin probably announced their relationship to anyone who was paying attention.

"Hi." Her skin prickled with awareness in his presence. Something about him lit her on fire, even out here in the everyday atmosphere of the market. She noticed a lime seller eyeing them curiously. "We should probably go somewhere else."

"I've been thinking about nothing but seeing you since yesterday." His eyes glittered with a desire that echoed her own.

"Me, too." It was hard to think straight with him around. Colors grew brighter and the sounds of the street seemed to blur into white noise. "I missed you."

She knew she was admitting too much, letting him know the power he had over her. He knew already, though. How could he not? She melted like butter in the hot sun whenever he was near.

"Let's walk." He gestured along the road that led south, toward the ocean. His hand twitched slightly and she could swear he wanted to put it around her waist, but was resisting.

They rounded the corner out of sight of the market stalls, and were now alone on a dusty street of modest houses. Quasar took her in his arms with a swiftness that almost pushed the breath from her lungs, and kissed her with intensity.

When their lips finally parted she was shocked for a moment at how bold he'd been to kiss her in public. "We shouldn't do this. Someone might see."

"Let them." His blue eyes flashed defiance. "I don't care who knows how crazy I am about you."

"You're not the one whose reputation is already in tatters."

He laughed. "That's where you're wrong. You should see what the media says about me."

She'd forgotten about that. "I did. I looked you up on the internet after I learned your full name, remember? All the more reason I shouldn't be seen smooching you in public. If I had any sense I'd stay far away from you."

"Don't believe everything you read." He had the decency to look somewhat concerned. "They make most of that stuff up to sell magazines."

"Where there's smoke there's usually at least a spark of fire." She raised a brow. "The most recent stories were about you and Laura Larson. Apparently one minute you were planning your wedding, the next she was telling everyone she prefers to be single. Did you dump her?"

His mouth quirked into a wistful smile. "She dumped me."

"Were you heartbroken?"

He looked at her for a moment, then shook his head gently. "No. I enjoyed her company but I didn't feel the same kind of…intensity I feel with you."

"She's very beautiful."

"You're more lovely than she is."

"Okay, now I know you're toying with me."

"You are. She gets this weird wrinkle between her eyebrows when she's thinking. And she always glances to the left when she's telling a fib. She's almost always acting and I realized over time that she's not as interesting as most people think."

"Really?"

"Really. She's nice, but pretty kooky. Far too much drama on a daily basis."

"More than, say, my father calling your family sons of dogs?"

He laughed. "I asked for that by going to see him when you told me not to."

"Or maybe you actually like drama, and seek it out."

He was silent for a moment, contemplating what she'd said. A little frisson of alarm crept through her when she realized there might be more than a grain of truth in her words.

"I am something of a thrill seeker, but in sports, not in romance."

"Or so you'd like to believe." Were things getting too dull and predictable with their romance, making him want to stir the pot by approaching her father? "I told you to leave my house and promised I wouldn't see you again. Next thing I know, you're making love to me in my own bedroom. You're a bad influence." She was kidding, but only just.

She glanced up and down the street. A white car drove by. "We shouldn't hang around here. Let's walk like we have somewhere to go."

Quasar put his arm through hers and started walking. She wanted to tug her arm back, but he resisted when she tried. His powerful muscles were hard to argue with.

"I'm a good influence. I'm here to help you out of your cloister before you spend your life locked away in it."

"I'd probably be a lot safer locked away in a cloister."

"Safety is overrated." He shot a teasing glance at her. "Adventure is a lot more fun."

"Until you end up in the jaws of a lion."

He squeezed her gently. "I'll protect you."

"Unless you are the lion."

"Even then." He pressed a warm kiss to her cheek. Then he stopped and spun her to face him. "Come back to the United States with me."

"What?" She let his words echo inside her brain. His arms were now around her waist, possessive, holding her steady so she couldn't move. Couldn't leave.

"I mean it. I'm planning a move to the East Coast. Most likely Boston. There's some top technical talent there that I want to leverage for one or other of my newest business ideas."

"MIT is there."

"Exactly. And Harvard. Harvard must have an art program or museum of some kind where you could find a job."

"Oh, I'm sure I can walk right into a curatorial position at Harvard." She chuckled. His idea was so outrageous that it was funny rather than scary.

"You think I'm kidding? If you worked at Princeton, you can work at Harvard."

"I was very lucky to get the position at Princeton. I was an idiot to give it up."

"Have you ever been to Boston?"

"Sure. I've attended a couple of conferences there. I even lectured at one. I talked about Mesopotamian metalworking techniques."

"Did you like the city?"

"Uh, sure."

He was serious. At least the look in his eyes said so. "It's not as big and bustling as New York or L.A., but I like that about it. And there are some lovely neighborhoods in the older parts of the city."

She blinked, still not really sure this was happening. "So, in your vision, we'd live together in Boston?"

"Yes." He squeezed her. "I can see us in a pretty brick house with a garden."

No mention of marriage, of course. Did he anticipate that she'd be happy shacking up with him, no commitment in sight? On the other hand she was not at all keen to venture into marriage again. It was probably safer to keep the exit door open at all times by keeping any partnerships free of legally binding obligations to stay together until death did them part.

"What about when you get tired of me?" She tried to inject a note of humor but it fell rather flat. Because she truly wanted to know the answer.

"Tired of you? Impossible." He squeezed her again, and her heart leapt. The kiss he pressed to her lips flushed her with heat and passion that made it impossible to think straight.

"How can you say that when you barely know me?" It was hard to remember that they'd only known each other a few days. Things had happened so fast between them.

"Instinct. And I've learned to trust my instincts. They rarely fail me."

She sighed. This was all a bit much to take in. "Outrageous as your idea sounds, I like it." Warning bells and alarms flashed in her mind. Was she really going to place her trust in a man and venture off into unknown territory with him, away from friends and family?

Possibly. She'd have to carefully consider all the pros and cons.

Quasar was already grinning. "Sensible woman. Salalah is lovely, but it's no place for a woman with a great career in art history ahead of her. And we'd come back regularly to visit."

We'd come back regularly. The *we* got her attention. He was thinking of them as a couple. Which shouldn't sound so odd since they were a couple.

She took in a deep steadying breath. It was really too perfect. Too good to be true. Surely she was missing something?

"What if it takes me a long time to find a job? I have very little left in my savings. Probably the plane flight alone would finish them off, and then…" She didn't relish the prospect of being financially dependent on a man again. It was probably the most effective way her ex-husband had exerted control over her—cutting off her income source and preventing her from finding another.

He looked thoughtful for a moment. "I'll offer you a fifty-thousand-dollar grant to research the frankincense trade in Salalah. How does that sound?"

"Like you're trying to buy my consent."

"Nonsense. It's purely academic curiosity that prompts me."

She tried to look like she was thinking it over. "There's some excellent scholarship in that field already."

"But I'd imagine that advances in technology allow satellite analysis that could reveal more lost settlements like Saliyah."

She frowned. "You might have a point."

"Think it over." He pressed another soft, warm kiss to her lips, then pulled his arms from around her waist and continued down the street. She hurried to catch up. Her mind spun so fast it was hard to walk at the same time. Her father would be sure to protest but if she could reassure him that she had "grant" money and he didn't have to support her, she might mollify at least some of his objections. And if she decided to go—if she really thought it was for the best—he could hardly stop her.

Quasar's wild scheme was entirely doable. It could transform her life instantly.

Or be the biggest mistake she'd ever made.

"I will think about it."

"Good. And if your thoughts aren't heading in the right direction, then call me and I'll set them back on the right course." His effortless confidence was both inspiring and a little infuriating. Oh, to possess some of that herself.

And the truth was, the more time she spent with Quasar, the more confident and optimistic she felt. Just the fact that she'd gone to look for a job today was a big step forward from lounging around her bedroom feeling like a loser. She'd once had big dreams—and the prestigious job she'd dreamed of—and maybe it wasn't too late to pursue them again.

She was starting to feel like her old self: the college

student who thought anything was possible. "I think I should go home now."

"Already? We only just met. I need to stare into your beautiful eyes for at least another half hour before I go live on memories for the rest of the day and night."

She giggled. "I can't think straight. What you suggested is so huge that it's taking over my brain. I have to make up a list of pros and cons."

"Cons? There aren't any."

"It's certainly hard to think of them when I'm standing here with you. That's why I need to go home."

He smiled, then shrugged. "Okay. I'll drive you home to dream up some cons. And maybe we can make love in your bedroom again."

"No way! I can't believe my brother almost caught us together in there. Never again. Really, I mean it!" She was talking too loud and looked about quickly to see if anyone had heard.

Quasar pretended to pout. "So cruel. But okay, I'll be good and drop you off if you promise to come to an event at the hotel this evening. It's Kira's fifth birthday party but it's for the grown-ups as much as the kids. Salim's hired a bunch of carnival acts to walk around the hotel and entertain people, and practically everyone in Salalah is invited."

"That alone is a good reason for me not to come. I don't want to become the subject of gossip."

"We'll tell people we're old friends." He grinned. "They'll just assume that since we were both in the U.S. that we bonded over there."

"What will I tell my father?" She frowned and shook her head. "Geez, I feel like a teenager. I can't believe I even have to think about this. I'll just tell him I'm going to visit a friend."

"Invite him to come, too." Quasar grinned.

"I'm sure he'd love that. Into the den of the Al Mansurs."

"You never know. People pull out all the stops to get invited to some of Salim's exclusive parties. He might surprise you."

"I don't think so. He's depressingly predictable." What would he say if she announced she was moving away with Quasar? She couldn't even imagine. If he were angry enough he could cast her out of the family and refuse to ever speak to her again. She hoped he'd never do that but there was no way to know for sure. She certainly wasn't going to breathe a word about it until she'd made up her own mind that moving to Boston with Quasar was a good idea. "I'll try to come, though. What time?"

"Five. It's early because of the kids."

"Okay. I'll come for a while and then go home for dinner."

"I could come pick you up."

"No! It's barely a twenty-minute walk. I'll see you there."

They walked to where his car was parked a couple of blocks away, and he took her home. Once again he drove around the back. There would have been plenty of time for her to invite him in but she was glad he didn't suggest it again.

She kissed him for a solid minute before climbing warily out of the car. She was reluctant to leave him. To wake up and find this was all a figment of her imagination. A dream that crept over her during an afternoon nap.

She could hardly believe he'd asked her to move back to the U.S. with him.

That meant this wasn't a fling but the start of something real.

Once inside the back door, she waved and watched him drive away.

With a sigh, she walked from the back of the house to the front and went to put her keys on the hall table, as if she'd come in the front door like a normal person with nothing to hide.

And that's when she saw her father and her brothers standing in the kitchen, right next to the window that looked out onto the street.

Nine

"What is the meaning of this, Daniyah?" Her father's lips grew white as he stared at her.

She could tell he'd seen Quasar. She didn't know what to say.

"Of what?"

"Don't treat me like a fool. Apparently you forgot I took your brothers to the engineering symposium at the university today. It was over by two and we returned to find you gone. You've been out with that…man."

"Only to the market. I bought some almonds." She held up the bag she'd almost forgotten about. "We didn't do anything else." For once, it was the truth.

His eyes started to bulge as his face reddened. "No? What else have you done with him on other occasions? You told me you weren't going to see him again. Clearly you lied to me so now I'm wondering what else is untrue. If your mother were alive today…!" He shook his head and exhaled as if he were going to breathe fire. "Perhaps I should forbid you to leave the house. I literally cannot believe that you were out walking around Salalah in broad daylight with one of those accursed Al Mansurs."

The mention of her mother chastened Dani. Who knew where they'd all be if her mother were alive. Dani would likely never have moved to the United States, or met Gordon. She'd probably have been fixed up by her mom and aunts with a nice, quiet Omani man, who didn't have flashing blue eyes or a reputation as an international playboy.

"I'm thinking of moving to America with him."

She said the words entirely without premeditation. They slipped out of her mouth as she was testing them in her mind.

Her father stared at her, speechless. Then his eyebrows started to twitch. "Have you taken leave of your senses?"

"You said yourself that I won't be able to find a job here. My skills may seem useless in Salalah, but I have a prestigious academic background and I was a curator at Princeton. In America my skills are far more marketable, especially in a university town like Boston."

"Boston? You've actually discussed this with him?" Her father's voice was hoarse with incredulity.

"Yes. Just today, in fact. I told him I'd think about it." She sounded surprisingly calm. Much calmer than she felt. She hadn't even had a chance to think this plan through properly and already she was announcing it almost as a done deal.

Her youngest brother stared, openmouthed. The other one stared at her through slightly narrowed eyes as if afraid he'd be blinded by what he was witnessing.

"Has he proposed marriage?"

"No." There wasn't really anything she could add to make this sound better. By Omani standards he probably should have proposed before they even kissed, certainly before they moved in together. She could say they were "just friends," but that would be a lie and she didn't want to make things worse by lying.

"How will you support yourself over there? Are you to be a kept woman?"

She wanted to mention the grant, but on reflection that probably would make her a kept woman. "I have enough savings left to get there. Then I'll find a job. Maybe not my ideal one, at first, but I'll find something."

"While living with this man?"

"I'm not a virgin, dad. I was married before."

"To your discredit." His bushy eyebrows lowered. "And now your own opinion of yourself is so low that you plan to willingly live in sin?"

"It's not like that in the States. It's quite normal for adults to live together for a while before they marry. To test each other out, really. If I'd done that before I married Gordon I probably could have saved myself a world of grief."

"I don't know you. I don't know who you are." He stood there, panting slightly. "You are not the daughter I raised."

His words cut her to the quick and she felt tears rise in her throat. "I'm just trying to do what's best for me. I don't even know if I should move to Boston. I'm thinking it through."

"You should move to Boston." His voice was calm and firm. "There is no place for you here. You are a bad influence on your brothers."

She glanced at them. Mute and horrified, they didn't even meet her gaze. Was she really a bad influence on them? With one failed marriage behind her and an illicit affair going on under their noses, she could hardly recommend herself as an example to follow. Her hands were starting to tremble. She wasn't ready for this. She'd meant to ponder her options, to plan and prepare and gear herself up for any inevitable showdown.

Right now she felt as if her life were exploding in her face and she needed to get out of here. She turned back to the door and slipped out, before the conversation could spiral any further downhill. There was no sense talking to her father when his temper was running so high he couldn't think straight. If she stayed he might do something drastic, like lock her in her room and take away her phone. It was better to escape while she still could.

Moving to Boston wasn't such a crazy idea. Her father had given her almost no choice. Although she realized there were risks inherent in going with Quasar—he readily admitted that he got bored easily, and he had a playboy reputation—if she could get her career going again she'd be fine by herself if the relationship fell apart.

Not sure where to go, she headed first for the familiar bookshop where she'd met Quasar. Thumbing through the soft pages of an old history book soothed her nerves. It was now late afternoon and since her father was already mad at her she had no reason not to go to the party.

She walked along the quiet streets with a growing sense of resolve. Her time of rest and recuperation was nearing its end and she was ready to get back in the swim of life.

The walk to the hotel took almost half an hour and it was odd walking through the grand hotel gates on foot, rather than arriving in a luxury car, but the staff welcomed her almost as if they recognized her—maybe they acted like that with all the guests?—and she soon found herself in the large, music-filled central courtyard surrounded by at least three hundred people, including jugglers, sword swallowers, even a snake charmer. Excited children darted about in their smartest party clothes, and their parents laughed and talked and watched them fondly.

The festive atmosphere further boosted Dani's mood and she looked eagerly about for Quasar. He'd be thrilled that she'd decided to come to Boston with him. Maybe they could even talk about booking the tickets and some of the logistics of the move?

She scanned the area around the fountain—which bubbled right now in a rainbow of LED colors—looking for his face in the crowd. At last she spotted Sara walking with Elan, who carried a sleepy little Hannah in his arms.

Dani greeted them with relief. "I'm looking for Quasar. I can't seem to find him."

Sara glanced at Elan. He cleared his throat. "Hmm. I'm not exactly sure where he is." He looked around the sea of partygoers. "Would you like me to go find him for you?"

"Oh, no. I'll find him myself, eventually. I can always call him on my phone as a last resort." She patted the phone in her pocket. Elan glanced at Sarah again before they smiled and moved away. Dani got an odd feeling from the way they looked at each other. Almost as if they were trying to communicate without her figuring something out. Suddenly the music seemed louder and the bustle and thrust of people rather disorienting.

She drew in a breath and headed for the other side of the courtyard, where tables were set up to serve drinks. She accepted a glass of pinkish lemonade from a waiter and was about to turn back to the crowd when she spotted Quasar under a colonnade off to the side of the courtyard. He appeared to be talking to someone who was hidden by a carved stone column.

A smile spread across her face as she headed toward him. But her enthusiasm cooled when she noticed the serious expression on his face. His gaze was intently focused on the person in front of him. Dani's pace slowed when she realized that he was talking to a woman who gripped both his hands in hers. She could see gold bangles on her wrists, and gold rings on long, elegant fingers.

Her gut crawled with unease. She paused and sipped her lemonade. Maybe she shouldn't intrude. She could just wait until he was done with this conversation. She tried to tug her attention away from him and back to the festivities, but her eyes kept swiveling back to the shadowed arches of the colonnade where he stood with the strange woman. It was odd that he hadn't glanced up and seen her yet, considering all the nervous energy she must be sending in his direction. His attention was riveted on this woman, who still clutched him like a life raft.

Keeping her eyes on a nearby knot of children watching a magician pull a string of colored scarves from his mouth, she moved a few steps closer, ears straining to catch some of Quasar's conversation.

"Oh, darling, you always kill me with that mysterious Arabian charm of yours." The woman's voice was rich and full, confident, too.

"I'm not Arabian. I'm Omani." He said it with a smile.

"I know that, silly. I'm here in Oman, aren't I? Crazy long flight, too. You know how that airplane air dries out my skin, but I did it all for you."

Dani glanced at them in time to see one of the ringed hands rove up his forearm, reaching over the cuff of his elegant shirt. She froze. Now she could see the familiar profile, topped with expensively coiffed blond hair. This was Laura Larson, screen goddess, and one of the many glamorous women Dani had seen pictured on his arm when she did her internet search.

She wondered if she should turn and disappear back into the crowd. But wasn't this the man she'd just resolved to move across the world with? Curiosity and a growing sense of alarm propelled her forward, even while her instincts cued her to flee. Even when she was only fifteen feet away, he still hadn't looked up and noticed her. His famous companion was keeping him fully occupied with a giggly account of her appearance two nights ago at an awards ceremony, where she'd had too much to drink.

"Hello, Quasar." Dani said it quietly during a momentary break in the conversation. She didn't want to get any closer without announcing herself. She already felt like an intruder.

He glanced up and smiled. Relief swept over her. For a moment she'd wondered if he'd even acknowledge her. "I came to the party," she said, pointlessly. "The kids are really enjoying it."

Quasar ignored her blathering. "Dani, this is Laura. Laura, Dani."

Laura thrust out a hand with sharp-looking nails and Dani managed to produce a reasonably firm handshake and a smile. "Nice to meet you," she said, though it wasn't nice at all. She'd come here excited to tell Quasar that she'd decided to move to Boston with him. And the presence of Laura Larson made that impossible.

"What brings you to Oman?" Dani couldn't resist asking.

"Quasar, of course. Is there any other reason for visiting such a tiny and faraway country?" Laura tossed her luxurious gold hair and shone an adoring glance on Quasar.

"You flatter me, but Dani knows that Oman's charms far outshine mine."

Laura gave Dani the once-over, then looked back at Quasar. Dani became self-conscious of her Omani attire. Laura herself had on a slinky cream dress with a plunging neckline that revealed her spray-tanned boobs, gold high-heeled sandals and a necklace of what looked like gold nuggets.

"Do people here not drink alcohol?" Laura surveyed the crowd.

"Not really." Quasar winked at Dani, which gave her a pleasant conspiratorial feeling. "It's a Muslim country. It's served to guests at the hotel who want it, though. Would you like a drink?"

"Absolutely, darling. I'm parched and this Shirley Temple they gave me isn't doing anything for my jet lag. A whisky sour would be a dream."

"Dani, would you like anything?"

"I'm fine, thanks."

"I'll be right back."

Quasar headed for the bar, leaving Dani with Laura. Awkward! "Do you work at the hotel?" Laura inquired while looking over her shoulder at the crowds.

"No. I'm a friend of Quasar's." She lifted her chin as she said it. Now would be the perfect time to announce she was about to move in with him, but prudence prevented her. She knew this woman was one of his ex-lovers. And she'd come all the way to Oman to see him. They were obviously still on friendly terms.

Maybe their relationship wasn't even over.

"Are you one of the girls whose hearts he broke when he was a ridiculously dashing teen heartthrob?"

"No. We met recently." She could see Laura's curiosity growing, and decided that being mysterious was the best policy. No need to even let on that she recognized her. Which was petty, since she quite liked her movies. Oh, well, she was jealous of Laura right now and that was making her petty. At least she could acknowledge it.

But it was rather scary to see herself grow green claws over Quasar. How was she going to feel in Boston when he had business meetings with women, or even social gatherings and networking? He was an outgoing, friendly and popular guy, so she'd better get used to sharing him if their relationship was going anywhere. "How do you know him?"

"Oh, Quasar and I go way back." Laura inhaled her pink mocktail like it was a shot of rum. "He's like the brother I never had." The platonic reference was strangely reassuring. "But who I sleep with!" Laura let out a giggle. "He's irresistible. What can I say?"

Dani swallowed. What could she say? Hopefully Laura didn't intend to sleep with Quasar tonight. But if she did, what exactly could Dani do about it if Quasar were ready, willing and able?

Where was Quasar? She turned and saw him returning with three tall glasses. "Whiskey sours for everyone." He handed Laura hers, then gave one to Dani.

She looked at it suspiciously. She didn't really drink. Apart from any religious objections, she was a total lightweight.

Quasar took a sip of his and Laura took a few refreshing gulps of hers. "Quasar, darling, you should come down under for my next shoot." She grabbed Quasar's shoulder. "It's near Melbourne, which is such a fantastic city. Beaches, nightlife, fun people."

"Sounds like Salalah." Quasar winked again at Dani. The gesture warmed and relaxed her.

"Have you been to Australia, darling?" She squeezed his shoulder.

"Never have."

"Come then, you'll love it. I promise."

This is where Quasar should have protested that he couldn't because he was about to move to Boston with Dani. But he didn't.

"Maybe I will. There's an interesting biotech firm in Sydney I've been keeping tabs on. I might come down and eyeball the place."

"Wonderful." Her hand rose up to cup his cheek. Dani tried not to squirm and spill her whiskey sour. "When shooting wraps, we can take a Jeep across the outback. I've always wanted to do that!"

How could Quasar let this strange woman fondle him right in front of her after all they'd shared over the last few days? He was acting as if Laura was his girlfriend and she, Dani, was his old and platonic friend. Which is of course what he'd said he would do to protect her reputation. Was he just trying to deflect attention from her by pretending Laura was still his lover?

"Laura surprised me today," he said to Dani. "She showed up unannounced with about forty pieces of luggage."

"Oh." Dani nodded. That was not at all reassuring. He obviously wouldn't have invited her to come here tonight if he'd known Laura was arriving.

This situation was uncomfortable. Not only was he trying to convince everyone else they were "just friends," he apparently wanted Laura to think that too. Dani decided to take the hint and make her exit at the first available opportunity.

"Forty pieces of luggage! There aren't even eight. And I had no idea what the climate would be like here. Deserts can be quite freezing at night. I wonder if the outback gets cold at night. I could bring a light fox fur." She giggled again.

Dani's drink was sweating in her hand and she was tempted to drink it just for something to do, but she worried that she might cough and splutter at the disgusting taste of whiskey. She had no idea what to say and was beginning to wish that the shining marble tiles of the floor would slide apart and allow her to sink gracefully into oblivion.

Mercifully, Salim announced over the mike that it was time to sing "Happy Birthday," and the crowd moved in toward where a giant, multilayer cake, iced with rainbow-colored unicorns, stood in the middle of the courtyard.

Dani made a dive for the exit and didn't look back to see if Quasar had noticed. This was possibly the most embarrassing experience of her life. Luckily only she knew that. Laura—even Quasar himself—had no idea she'd come here to tell Quasar of her plans to go back to the States with him. To live with him and accept his generous offer to support her, which basically would have made her a kept woman.

Kept by a man for whom she was just one of many women whose company he enjoyed.

Thank goodness she'd seen Quasar's true colors and come to her senses. She put her drink down on a table as she passed out of the large courtyard, unnoticed amongst the joyous crowd singing "Happy Birthday" in several languages at the same time. She felt like a killjoy that she couldn't at least celebrate his niece's birthday, but tears were dangerously close to the surface and she needed to get out of here before they erupted.

It was over. Her exhilarating romance with Quasar. Her bold plans for starting over again in Boston. All of it. Now she was right back where she'd started except that now her father thought she was a loose woman as well as a foolish one.

She managed to keep a straight face as she hurried past the army of valets and bellhops and maintenance staff, striding along the wide driveway that led out the hotel gates. Out on the main road she kept going, walking as fast as she could. The chiffon fabric of her clothing kept catching on itself, and she cursed the fact that traditional Omani women's wear consisted of both a dress and pants. Maybe it was planned that way to make it harder for a woman to escape from her lover in a moment of crisis.

She should be glad, really. Her brain raced and her breathing got faster as she strode down the dusty sidewalk. She'd been saved from the humiliation of embarking on yet another disastrous live-in relationship with a totally unsuitable man. She'd just have to accept the truth that she had awful taste in men. She needed to find some kind of job where she could support herself, move out and get a cat for companionship.

She'd hoped the walk home would clear her head and settle her emotions; instead the first tears fell as she rounded the corner into her neighborhood. She wiped them hurriedly away with her scarf. Would her father even let her back in the house or would she be ordered to leave the way Quasar had been when he showed up?

She bit her lip and fought back the tears. The walk had flown by so quickly on her way to the party when she was filled with excitement and hope for the future. Now she prayed she wouldn't run into her neighbors out for an evening stroll. She couldn't bear to see anyone right now.

Why hadn't Quasar kissed her? If he had she'd probably have been shocked, and worried about her reputation, and scolded him. But now the fact that he hadn't made her feel like a castoff. His conspiratorial winks had suggested that they were still a team in some sense. Just not in any public sense where he'd claim her as his actual girlfriend.

Had she really thought Quasar was going to take her to America as his sweetheart? The idea seemed ridicu-

lous. She'd been swept away on a tide of lust and anticipation and started thinking that anything was possible.

Just the way she had in her marriage. If she'd thought
it all through, as her friends suggested, she'd have realized from the start that Gordon was already insecure and
controlling. Warning signs were flashing almost from
their first date. His obsessive questions about where she'd
been and who she'd seen. His preference for her to wear
modest clothing and avoid makeup. His enthusiasm for
spending every spare minute with her. She'd taken them
as signs that he was crazy about her, had traditional val-
ues and was going to be a wonderful and doting husband.

She'd been right about one part—he was crazy.

She turned onto her block and cringed at the sight of
three of her male neighbors talking in the street. They'd
probably mutter under their breath about this wayward
woman out and about without a male escort. She lifted
her head and smiled, though, and they greeted her. She'd
better be polite to everyone, as currently staying here was
her best-case scenario, and if she had any sense she'd be
grateful to have a roof over her head.

She'd have to apologize to her father. Tell him he was
right.

Tears still pricked at her eyeballs and she wanted nothing more than to let them flow down her cheeks again.
Her heart clenched at the thought that her lovely romance
with Quasar was nothing but a brief fling. Even though
she'd been telling herself that all along, trying to protect
her heart from this kind of pain.

"Back so soon?" Her father opened the door before
she even had a chance to try her key. He must have seen
her coming down the street. "Your lover didn't even have
the decency to drive you home?"

"He's not my lover." Her voice wore a heavy tone of resignation.

"No? I thought that you intended to live in sin with him in America."

"Not anymore." The confession seemed to sap her last ounce of energy.

"He's turned you away already?" The gleam of triumph in her father's eye made her heart sink further.

The question was so cold and mean that she decided not to answer it. She couldn't even bring herself to apologize. She simply walked toward him, where he stood blocking the hallway to her room, and prayed he'd let her go there in peace. "May I go to my room?" she asked softly.

"Don't disgrace the family." She'd expected a cold retort, but the sad look in her father's eyes cut her even deeper. Then he moved aside to let her pass.

He was trying to do the right thing, from his perspective. She had to remember that. He was afraid that she'd ruin her reputation and be a burden to him for the rest of his life. Maybe he was right to worry. All her exciting prospects for the future had dried up within the last hour.

Quasar hadn't officially dumped her. Not yet, anyway. He probably had his hands full with Laura Larson and wouldn't get to that for the next few days. And maybe not even then. He'd be busy planning his trip to Australia and the sex-filled romp across the outback with Laura wearing her fox fur over nothing but lacy lingerie.

Jealous! She cursed herself for her hateful feelings. Laura Larson hadn't done anything to her except be gorgeous and charming and bubbly and wildly successful. She had no idea she was stealing someone else's man, since she obviously saw Quasar as hers. The proprietary way she'd touched and fondled him left no doubt.

And he'd hardly slapped her hand away like it was an irritant.

In her room, Dani locked the door and carried her laptop to her bed where she sat and opened it with shaking fingers. She needed information. She wanted to see if she could find out how long Quasar and Laura had been together and if there was any further information about their relationship.

She entered their names, quietly hoping for news of a dramatic and tear-filled breakup. Instead she was confronted with picture after picture of them, dressed in stylish clothing at red carpet affairs, dancing together at hot L.A. nightclubs, on Rollerblades at Venice Beach, even shopping together at Whole Foods like a married couple.

Her heart descended further into her chest cavity. She wasn't in the least bit cheered to learn that Laura was twelve years older than Quasar and almost twenty years older than her. Who cared? She looked fabulous and was clearly living life to the fullest. Laura Larson was a woman in control of her own destiny, not one sitting around as an unwelcome guest in her father's house, wondering if she'd ever earn a single penny again, let alone fulfill all her dreams of romance and riches.

Laura Larson Dumps Young Lover, blared one headline. It didn't mention Quasar by name but it was recent and the description—"sexy entrepreneurial sheikh"—fit him to a T. In the article, Laura explained, and Dani could almost hear her giggling as she read it, that she needed to focus on her new role in an upcoming space opera blockbuster. In another article a week later there was speculation that she was dating George Clooney. Then rumors of an affair with Leonardo DiCaprio swirled. Dani began to wonder if Laura's publicist was just sending out press releases to boost her profile, while she was still quietly enjoying the many pleasures of Quasar's company.

He probably didn't care what the tabloids said. He was too busy buying and selling billion-dollar companies and drinking thousand-dollar bottles of champagne.

And making passionate love to Laura Larson.

A tear dripped down onto her keyboard and she cursed her self-pity. She should be congratulating herself on a narrow escape. She could have uprooted herself and gone to Boston with him, only to find herself abandoned while he headed off to enjoy Laura, or any of the other beauties he'd dated before. Or someone new.

He'd flirted with Dani so readily and seduced her so quickly that it was almost ridiculous. Especially as she had good reason to be wary of men! He must possess almost hypnotic powers over women, and they'd certainly worked on her. It was hard to believe that she of all people had allowed him not only to kiss her, but also to seduce her into bed.

Had she lost her mind?

Her phone chimed and made her jump. Was it him? She couldn't resist checking.

Where are you?

She frowned. Had he just noticed that she'd gone missing from the party? It must be nearly an hour since she'd left. He'd probably been so busy with Laura running her hands all over him that he hadn't realized Dani wasn't there for the cake cutting.

She put the phone facedown on the comforter and went back to her laptop screen. Looking at more pictures of him and Laura would save her from weakening. He was all wrong for her. He'd break her heart.

She bit her lip when she realized it was probably already too late to avoid getting her heart broken. She'd become attached to him so quickly, that it was already hard to imagine her life without him

Her phone chimed again. She tried to summon the strength to leave it facedown on her bed. She failed and picked it up, heart racing.

Dani, I've been looking for you everywhere.

I left the party. She'd typed a reply before she could stop herself. And why shouldn't she tell him? It was the truth. She'd have to tell him that she wasn't moving to Boston with him, and why, as well, so there was no point in totally avoiding him.

Though it was essential to keep enough distance that he couldn't work his hypnotic charms on her as usual.

I can see that.

She bit her lip. She wanted to type *I miss you, too,* but that was some foolish part of her that got swept up in a romantic fantasy that had little to do with what was really going on between them. She put the phone down again and stood staring at it, with her arms crossed, as if daring it to try something.

How did you slip away?

She watched the words appear on the screen, from her safe vantage point a few feet away. Her brain supplied an answer: *It wasn't hard. You didn't even notice me leave.*

She didn't type that, either.

I need to see you.

Had he decided he preferred her to Laura? Did he now want to apologize for acting as if Laura and he were an item at the party? Or did he just want to keep Dani warm on the back burner in case he wanted some steamy sex later that week.

It was sad how quickly her optimistic, romantic glow had turned cynical.

Will you meet me?

She drew in a deep breath and approached the phone as if it were a snake that might bite her if handled wrong. No.

Did he really think she'd want to see him after he let Laura paw him at the party? He must live in a world of illusion. Then again, of course he did. He'd grown up as one of the storied Al Mansurs, with their millions in oil wealth and everything handed to them on a platter. He was used to women bowing at his feet and doing whatever he wanted.

She'd certainly done it easily enough, and she hadn't even known who he was at first.

Dani half waited for him to text again, explaining that Laura meant nothing to him, and she—Dani—was the only woman he cared about. That was probably beneath his dignity, though. He'd certainly never mentioned his other woman friends to her. Likely he thought them none of her business.

Are you at home?

She hesitated for a moment, holding the phone in her hand. If she told him she was at home he'd probably come over, and embarrass her even further in front of her father and brothers.

Her fingers twitched to reply. She could vividly picture Quasar typing on his phone and being confused and possibly hurt by her brusque responses. She didn't want to hurt him. She cared about him. Her feelings for him were confusing and intense and she'd almost begun to think they might be that elusive and dangerous thing she'd once called love.

She wasn't falling down that rabbit hole again, though. Her heart wanted to text Quasar back. To make plans to meet with him. To fall into his arms, to believe whatever he promised and float along on a rose-scented cloud of bliss for as long as she could.

But she'd tried that approach to life once. Ignoring warning signs. Being nice. Hoping for the best. Smoothing things over when they got rocky. Trying to save everyone's feelings but her own. And she wasn't doing that again.

Ever.

Then she heard a knock on her window.

Ten

The sound of knuckles rapping on the glass made Dani jump and drop her phone. She spun around and a barrage of confusing emotions assaulted her as she saw Quasar's face emerge from the evening gloom outside her window: relief that he cared enough to come; horror that once again he'd ignored etiquette to pursue her; and fear that she'd fall immediately under his seductive spell.

He knocked again, more softly this time, to draw her from her frozen indecision. She realized she had to open the window. After yesterday's experience of being stuck in her room with the bars locked from the outside, she'd found the key and snuck it into her desk drawer. She drew it out, pulled up the window sash—pressing her finger to his lips to warn him into silence—and handed it to him.

He slid the key into the lock at the bottom of the barred grating. She watched his moonlight-dusted profile, sharp cheekbones, proud nose, characteristically tousled hair. Looking at him made a girl forget about common sense and what was right.

The lock clicked open and he lifted the large, heavy iron grid that hinged from the top, eased himself under it and opened the window. In a few brief seconds, he was inside her room and standing on her carpet.

"You can't stay," she whispered. "My father and brothers are home."

"I know. Come with me." He gestured at the window with his chin.

She shook her head silently. She could hear the TV from down the hall. Al Jazeera news on full volume. It was unlikely that anyone would hear them if they kept their voices down. "We can talk here," she said softly. "It's time to end this madness and go back to our separate lives."

"You can't be serious." He stepped toward her and seized hold of her hands. "A few hours ago you liked the idea of coming with me."

"That was before I saw you with Laura." The confession was an instant weight off her mind. That was the true reason she'd changed her mind—totally and irrevocably—about moving to Boston with him. She'd caught a glimpse of the real Quasar, in his own element, and felt like the outsider she would be if she were foolish enough to try living with him.

He squeezed her hands and she felt an echoing squeeze in her heart. "Dani. Laura was important to me. That's all over. Now she's simply an old friend."

"I think she wants to be a lot more than friends."

"She's very touchy-feely, but she's really like that with everyone. Besides, it doesn't really matter what she wants. I know what I want and that's you."

Dani swallowed. She wished he wasn't holding her hands so tightly so she could pull away and put some space between them.

"Maybe you can't admit to yourself that you really want her back."

She saw the familiar twinkle of humor in his eyes. She wasn't sure whether to be reassured that he found her worries amusing, or appalled that he could find humor even when she was trying to dump him.

"I don't want her back. I don't like to talk about past relationships, as I think it's more respectful to both parties to keep everything private, but I was relieved when our relationship ended. I don't want a woman who lives to see and be seen, and who gets restless if she stays in one city for more than two weeks. I want someone calming and steady, whose resources come from within and who prefers peace and intimacy to a glittering crowd." He squeezed her hands again and took another step closer until his chest was almost touching hers. "I want you."

Her heart leaped and she cursed it. The sincerity in his voice clawed at her. Now that they were alone together again, all her doubts and fears seemed to shrivel away and the grand hopes and dreams he inspired reinflated and threatened to warp her perspective. "I know you think that now. That you really believe it. But I felt like the outsider at that party, like she claimed you and owned you and I was an intruder. I know she's only one of many women you've dated, and I just can't compete with them. I don't want to. I'll be jealous and resentful and hate myself. Why didn't you tell her to take her hands off you?"

He frowned. "I should have. I was thoughtless and assumed too readily that you knew I was yours and only yours. From now on, no woman shall touch me but you." He lifted her hands to his mouth and kissed them.

A strange sensation shivered through her belly. "You can't promise that. What are you going to do? Beat them off with a stick?"

"If necessary." The look in his eyes suggested that he was entirely serious. "Or perhaps I can carry a *khanjar* at my belt and slice at them if they try."

She giggled. It was impossible not to. She could totally picture Quasar with the traditional dagger tucked into his Armani suit.

Then she stopped laughing. "I'm scared. Everyone who knows me will think it's wrong, that I've lost my mind."

"Do you listen to them, or to your heart?" His eyes narrowed, and he peered into hers with what looked like the wisdom of a thousand years.

"I listened to my heart before, and it was wrong. I thought I'd met my life partner and I tried to make it work but he was cruel and destructive to me. I don't trust my judgment anymore."

"I love you, Dani. I want you by my side. What will it take?"

She blinked, staring at him. Cool resolve crept over her. "If I'm not happy, you'll let me go, no questions asked?"

He frowned again. He seemed to be considering her words. "Though it would pain me to let you go, I'll agree."

"Even if I ask you to let me go right now?" This was the ultimate test. He'd refused once. Did he respect her enough to do what he promised?

He gave her a confused look. "You want me to leave right now?"

"And never come back."

His mouth moved, as if he were at a loss for words. "I can't promise that." His regal brow furrowed. "I can't."

"See? You can't promise you'll let me go. You want me to be yours, no matter what the cost to me. I've played by those terms once and I won't do it again." Her own determination strengthened as she stood up to him.

She watched his chest rise as he drew in a steadying breath. "You want me to leave you—forever—to prove how much I love you?"

What she asked didn't make any sense, but she was going to lose him either way. She couldn't go with him and plunge herself into a life of uncertainty. She nodded, her lips pressed together.

Quasar raised her hands to his lips again. His blue eyes were shadowed with darkness as he kissed them one more time—so softly—sending tremors of sensation and emotion to her toes. Then he bowed, turned to the window, climbed out and walked off into the night. Her heart breaking, she watched his white shirt disappear into the darkness.

He did it. He promised he'd let her go, and he did. And the worst part was that now she loved him more than ever.

Quasar's heart pounded so hard it could break a rib. He was glad of the brisk walk to where he'd parked his car a couple of blocks away. He understood where Dani was coming from. She'd been pushed around, told what to do, what not to do, and she had to be sure she was in charge of her own destiny.

As a man used to being in control of his life and that of many people around him, it didn't sit well at all to just walk away. It was hard enough to leave when he knew he'd see her the next day. Now she expected him to go back to his life and forget all about her?

No way.

He'd go back to his life—what there was of it without her in it—and breathe through each day until she came to her senses and claimed him. That was the only reason he'd been able to leave. He knew it was a test. It was easy to fail, very hard to pass.

And who knew how long the test would last?

He'd ached to wrap his arms around her and draw her into his embrace. His skin had crawled when Laura kept touching him earlier, but he'd never needed a strategy for keeping a woman at arm's length so he'd never developed one. From now on he'd wear invisible armor—projected in his bearing—that kept anyone but Dani from even touching him.

He wouldn't text her. He wouldn't call her. He wouldn't show up at her usual haunts, or hover outside her window like a ghost.

But he would win her back.

"You've taken leave of your senses," Salim growled. He rose to his feet and towered over his desk. "You've lost all perspective on reality."

"I love her."

Light blasted through the window of Salim's austere, white-walled office with its view out over the glittering ocean. Quasar had come to tackle an important hurdle on the road to winning Dani over.

"You love her so much that I need to take a piece of land worth millions—billions in future revenue—and simply give it away to a man I detest who's wasted untold hours of my time and thousands of rials with his meritless lawsuits."

"I'll buy the land from you at market value."

"The market value is in no way commensurate with the value that land has to me as the site of my future flagship hotel."

"Then I'll pay whatever value you set."

"Even if it's fifty million dollars?" Salim arched a brow. "That, in fact, is an approximate figure for my construction costs alone. I have big plans for this property."

"I won't be able to simply write a check for that amount. I'll have to free up some assets, but I can have the money for you by the end of next week. Tell me which account you'd like it transferred into." He pulled out his phone to type in the information.

"You really have taken leave of your senses."

"Quite the opposite, brother. I've finally come to my senses." He smiled.

"But she hasn't even agreed to marry you."

"I haven't asked."

"Why not?"

"Because she'd say no."

"If she doesn't want you, why would you risk fifty million dollars trying to win her favor?"

"She does want me." He cocked his head. "She's afraid of herself, though. She's afraid of making a poor choice. I have to prove to her than I'm an excellent choice, and I won't stop until I've done that."

Salim sighed, and sat back in his big leather chair. "I know how you feel, brother. I've been there myself. There's no pain more acute than the loss of a woman your happiness depends on."

"Elan told me that Sara would only come live with him if he agreed not to marry her. She didn't want to be trapped or tied down by convention. It seems that sometimes we Al Mansur men have to learn to let our women fly free before we can convince them to come nest with us."

Salim laughed. "And Celia made me sign a contract promising that she and Kira could leave whenever they wanted. But neither myself nor Elan had to pay fifty million dollars for the privilege of being with our wives."

"Daniyah Hassan is a very special woman. I've never felt the kind of peace and happiness I know in her arms. I had no idea it was even possible."

"That's sweet and romantic, brother, but I'm extremely attached to that piece of land. Why don't you give your princely sum to her father in exchange for it? I'm sure one million would buy him off with a smile, never mind fifty."

"Dani says her father won't take money for the land. The whole affair has dragged on so long that it's personal. He won't stop until he gets the land back."

"The courts would never side with him."

"Are you willing to wait twenty years for that outcome? Surely you can buy another piece of property. Maybe one of those big houses along the shore? Or perhaps Hassan will gladly sell it back to you for money once he's had the satisfaction of walking on it. I doubt he has any plans for it other than a quick sale."

"True. You can buy it from me for fifty million and give it to Hassan for nothing, then I'll buy it back from him for five. I'm suddenly seeing this as a very profitable venture." Salim grinned. "If you're really madly in love enough to go through with this, then may your sweetheart come running to you before you come back to your senses and realize how nuts this all is."

"Great." Quasar grinned back. "I'll need the SWIFT and IBAN numbers for the transfer."

"No need for all that fuss." Salim reached across the table and shook Quasar's hand firmly. "I'll take a check."

Dani returned from a trip to the local American school in an upbeat mood. She'd applied for an advertised position as a teacher's aide, and been told that she had a good shot at getting it. While assisting in a classroom wasn't the position she'd studied and trained for, it was a job and would provide income and independence to get her back on her feet. She was almost whistling with joy as the taxi dropped her off at the house.

"Dani!" Her heart sank when she saw her father in the

doorway with an anxious expression on his face. Uh-oh. He'd be angry that she'd gone out, yet again, without a male family member to escort her. She couldn't possibly expect to find a job, let alone keep one, if she had to wait until he or one of her brothers had the free time to take her somewhere.

"Something extraordinary has happened." His eyebrows were jumping all over the place. He didn't look angry, though. If anything he looked stunned.

"What is it?"

He waved a big brown envelope in the air. "A courier just delivered this package. It contains a deed to the property on Beach Road. And a contract that conveys the title back to me. All that I have to do is sign it and send a token ten rials to seal the deal."

"Ten rials? Is this a joke?"

"The token amount makes it legal. Quasar Al Mansur says he wants to gift the property to me outright and return it to our family."

Her mouth hung open. That property was worth millions. And she'd seen how passionate his brother Salim was about it. Had he persuaded his brother to part with it just because of her?

It didn't seem possible. "Let me see."

Her father handed her the envelope and she pulled out an old deed typed on yellowed paper. There was also a contract for the change of ownership, signed by Quasar and requiring her father's signature. The part that made her heart thud, however, was a letter from Quasar insisting that he wanted to return the land as a gesture of goodwill between their families.

He'd been true to his word and not contacted her since she sent him back out through her window three days earlier. She was impressed that he'd managed to obey her wishes, when he was clearly a man used to demanding—and taking—what he wanted.

She was even more impressed that she'd managed to stay strong enough not to call him herself. Her mind and body ached with missing him. At night she craved the feel of his arms around her—even though she'd never felt them around her at night, only during snatched sojourns in the heat of the day.

Taking time apart from him allowed her to breathe. To think. Now that she had time to ponder, she was glad she hadn't run away with him. They barely knew each other and what she knew about him was alarming. If she'd accepted his "grant," she would have basically been an expensive mistress, which wasn't how she wanted to start out her new life. She thought he'd soon get over their whirlwind affair and move on. She'd be just another in a long line of women he'd earnestly adored and left behind.

But discovering that he wanted to give her father a piece of land worth millions put an entirely different spin on the situation. It proved he was serious. Even if money was virtually no object for him personally, he'd had to persuade his brother to shelve his hotel plans—which couldn't have been easy—and he'd gone to the trouble of having the legal paperwork drawn up.

She looked up at her father. "Are you going to sign it?"

"Do you think it's a trick?"

"I don't know." She tried to focus but all the small print on the contract blurred in front of her eyes. "It certainly seems real. You should have a lawyer look over it."

"I don't trust those Al Mansurs. It could be some kind of trap. If I sign this paper allowing them to transfer the land to me, it will be like admitting that I never owned it in the first place. I'd be giving up my claim that I currently own the land."

"But if the contract is genuine you'd be giving it up in return for outright ownership of the land. Ten rials is a lot cheaper than the thousands of rials you'd have to pay to your lawyer to take your claim all the way through the courts."

"That is certainly true." Her dad rubbed his mustache with a finger.

"What would you do with the land?" Now that ownership of the property was within reach, her father seemed oddly lackadaisical about it. Which was strange, since he'd been gnashing his teeth over being "robbed" for as long as she could remember.

"Sell it, of course." His brows lifted, probably as he contemplated how much he could get for it.

"Maybe you could sell it back to Salim Al Mansur."

Her father's brows lowered. "Why would he give it to me for free only to buy it back? Maybe there's something I don't know. Maybe he's contaminated the land. He could have buried toxic waste on it. It seems too good to be true."

Like her relationship with Quasar. Too sudden, too easy, too fabulous, too far, too fast. She sighed. "I'm not sure we can ever truly understand other people's motivations. You just need to decide if you still really want it, and if you do, then get in touch with a lawyer and make sure all the documents say what they are supposed to say. If they do, then sign them, take your fishing rod to the land and catch some fish." She attempted a half smile. It couldn't really be that easy, could it?

No way. Nothing ever was.

Quasar didn't want to go back to the United States. His visit to Oman was stretching into its third week, but now that Dani wasn't coming with him, the prospect of moving to Boston and exploring the intriguing business opportunities there had palled. For one thing he'd miss these jovial breakfasts on the hotel veranda, where the whole family gathered together to start the day. Elan and Sara still showed no signs of returning to their home in Nevada, and he felt the same way about leaving.

He watched Celia's long fingers deftly wind a hair tie around the bottom of Kira's fishtail braid while the little girl munched on a blueberry muffin. Would he ever have children of his own to take care of? Since he'd met Dani, he'd thought about the prospect more than once.

Celia glanced up. "Salim told me about the land deal. When are you going back to propose marriage?"

Quasar ripped a croissant in half. "It's not a done deal yet. Dani's father has had the contract for two days and I haven't heard a word. Maybe he's so difficult he'll refuse to take the land back as a gift because he'd rather win it in court." His chest tightened as he thought about it. Could he lose his chance of a lifetime with Dani due to her own father's stubbornness?

So many pieces had to fall into place for this to work.

"It may well be a done deal, brother. A courier left a big envelope at the front desk for you this morning," Salim said.

"What?" Quasar leapt from his chair. "Why didn't you tell me?"

"I just did." Salim smiled enigmatically.

Quasar felt like punching him. Salim still hadn't cashed the damn check, either, which made the whole deal feel rather illusory since the contract gifting the land was between Quasar and Mohammed Hassan. He dialed the front desk and asked them to bring any mail to him. He glared at Salim. "You're enjoying this, aren't you?"

"Enormously. Who'd have thought that my baby

brother would be so madly in love with a woman that he'd part with fifty million dollars for the chance to win her favor."

"It is adorable." Sara smiled and smoothed a cowlick in Ben's hair. "But then you Al Mansurs are the biggest romantics once you finally fall in love."

One of the front-desk staff brought the envelope to the table and Quasar ripped into it with his heart pounding. There was the contract—signed and notarized—and a letter from Mohammed Hassan thanking him for recognizing his long-held claim to the land and returning it to its rightful owner. Quasar smiled. "It's all signed, sealed and delivered."

Salim shook his head. "I've never seen anyone so happy about parting with fifty million dollars *and* a prime piece of oceanfront real estate."

Quasar winked. "Thanks for making it possible."

"So now you can go back and propose." Celia looked at him down the length of her elegant nose.

"Not so fast!" Sara exclaimed. "Dani just extracted herself from a miserable marriage. It might be quite some time before she can be persuaded to go down that road again. If ever. Why does marriage have to be such an important part of every relationship? It's as if you can't enjoy being a couple until there's some legal paperwork saying you own the rights to each other in perpetuity."

Elan laughed. "See what I have to deal with? I did finally persuade her to marry me, though."

"How?" Quasar couldn't hide his curiosity.

Sara leaned forward. "By proving to me, day after day, that he really wanted to be with me, and enjoy my company, and share a family with me, not own me and control me and run me. You Al Mansurs may be successful but you've been raised with some bad habits that can need breaking."

"I don't want to own Dani or run her life."

"You don't think you do, but you do expect her to fall neatly into your plans. What if she wants to stay in Salalah rather than moving to Boston?"

He frowned. "I'm pretty sure she wants to move back to America."

"But if she didn't you'd be willing to stay here with her even if it means giving up on that biotech company you're all excited about acquiring?"

He thought for a moment about the considerable sacrifice required, then answered with conviction. "Yes. I have a strong feeling about it. Call it intuition, or a hunch, or maybe even destiny, but I truly believe Dani and I are meant to be together."

Elan leaned forward and clapped him on the back. "Then take your time and make sure you don't screw it up like I nearly did. Sara scared me so good I waited through her entire pregnancy with our son, and half of our first year as parents, before I even dared ask her again."

Sara looked at him lovingly. "Luckily by then I was ready to say yes."

"How soon before I can try to buy the land back?" Salim cocked his head. "I have plans drawn up and was waiting to resolve the title issues before submitting them for approval."

"If I can hold my horses, brother, you can, too." Quasar let out a sigh. "Patience may not be our strong suit but it builds character for us to apply it."

"Finding the right woman is what builds character most of all," Salim said quietly. "I was bulldozing my way through life trying to get everything so perfect that I almost destroyed my one chance at happiness. I consider myself the luckiest man alive that Celia was able to find it in her heart to forgive me for being such an utter ass."

Celia laughed. "The whole situation was character-building for me, too. I kept your daughter secret from you because I was too afraid you'd tried to seize control of her." She squeezed Quasar's arm. "But as you can see he managed to win me over, so hang in there and keep your goal in sight."

Elan leaned back in his chair. "It certainly sounds as if you've found a woman strong and steady enough to handle you, so take her needs seriously, and don't blow it. What do you plan to do next?"

"Propose to her."

Quasar guided his silver Mercedes through the now-familiar streets of Dani's quiet neighborhood, past the silent houses with their shuttered windows. Unfamiliar trepidation quickened his heartbeat. The next step was a big one, and he wasn't entirely sure how to handle it. Since he wasn't used to such uncertainty, the effect was decidedly unsettling.

Despite his brothers' experiences, he'd decided that Dani was obviously uncomfortable with the idea of accompanying him to America with her status in his life uncertain. So it was important to clarify that status. Which meant proposing marriage.

And since this was Oman, he also needed her father's permission. Right now he had no idea how either of them would respond to his proposal.

He parked his car directly in front of the house, announcing his arrival to anyone who happened to glance out a window. He half hoped someone would open the door and say something, so he could avoid the suspense of climbing the doorstep and knocking. He still remembered how badly his last visit had gone.

The difficult part was that he had to ask Dani to marry him first. He'd deliberately chosen to come here in the early evening, when her father and brothers were home, so everything would be proper and aboveboard and he couldn't be accused of sneaking around or trying to seduce her into bed. The snag was that if her father answered the door, how did he explain his purpose and ask to see Dani without either giving the game away or getting thrown out on his ear or…both?

It would take some cunning.

Dani had been at her computer since lunchtime, typing letters. Buoyed by her positive experience at the American school—from which a job offer seemed almost certain—she'd decided to broaden her horizons. She'd polished her resumé and written letters of introduction to five different universities with art history or history programs that featured a strong interest in Near Eastern art. She was putting the final touches on them and intended to sleep on them and, if she were still feeling bold enough, to email them out tomorrow morning. One of them was to a department at Harvard. Unlikely as it seemed, she was opening the door to going to Boston all by herself.

And all the activity kept her from thinking about Quasar, who had somehow engineered the return of her father's land.

She missed him so much that her belly ached. The urge to text him, just to say hi, was almost irresistible. She yearned to hear his deep, rich voice in her ear, even if it were only through her phone speaker. She wanted to speak with him about her plans and get his opinion of her letters. She craved his encouragement and support even as she told herself she could get along fine without it.

He'd been true to his word and let her go. And right now she felt like a complete idiot for letting him.

"Dani!" Her brother's voice accompanied his sharp knock on her door. "Dad's calling you."

She frowned. Why didn't he just come get her? Why send her brother? "Coming."

She saved her document and closed it. She'd been so busy and wrapped up in her plans she hadn't noticed it was nearly dinnertime. She washed her hands and smoothed her hair and tried not to laugh—or cry—at her lovelorn expression in the mirror. Two tiny dark smudges had formed under her eyes, making her look like a mournful maiden from an ancient miniature. Or a zombie. She sighed. Sooner or later she'd get over Quasar and the dark rings would go away again. She probably just needed more exercise.

"Dani, what's keeping you?" Her father's gruff voice startled her out of rubbing her fingers on her face and pinching color into her cheeks.

"I'm on my way. What's the rush?"

"We have a visitor."

"Who?"

"Come here." Maybe her aunt Riya had stopped by to say hello.

She turned into the hallway, and saw a tall silhouette just inside the door. Her heart started to pound. It was Quasar.

"Hello, Dani." That familiar, rough yet smooth voice sent excitement coursing through her.

"Hello, Quasar." She tried to sound cool and noncommittal as her blood heated several degrees. Why was he here? Should she be mad at him for breaking his promise to stay away, or thrilled that he cared enough to come back?

A broad smile widened her dad's mouth and his body language suggested that Quasar was an old friend rather than a sworn enemy with undesirable designs against his daughter. Apparently the priceless gift of oceanfront property had earned him a place in her father's heart. Had he done that for her?

"Come, Khalid and Jalil. Let's leave them in peace." Dani stared as her father ushered her brothers out into the garden, leaving her and Quasar alone in the house.

"What's going on?" She blinked, suddenly confused. She'd forgotten how tall he was, and how broad his shoulders were. The sight of him, blue eyes flashing, was enough to dazzle her completely.

"Dani." He took her hands, enveloping them in his. As usual, this action had a disturbing effect on her entire body. "I know you told me to stay away from you, and I did for as long as I could possibly stand. Now I'm going to ask you something very important and I want you to think carefully about your answer. What you say now will affect both of our lives, one way or the other, so take your time."

She stared at him. He must be about to propose marriage. What else would come with such dramatic foreshadowing? She'd have to say no, of course. They didn't know each other well enough.

And she was far too deeply in love to make any kind of rational decision about it.

"Why did you give my father the land?" The question had burned in her brain since she'd seen the contract.

"I wanted to solve a problem."

"But it wasn't your problem. It was between your brother Salim and my father." There was something so chivalrous about his attempt to bridge the divide between their two families. His efforts touched her deeply.

"It's important to me that both of them are happy. I sincerely hope I'll be able to make that happen."

"I can't believe you just gave it to him as a gift. It's worth...I have no idea what it's worth." More than a million, for sure. She tried to rein in her enthusiasm. Quasar had done all this behind her back, without her knowledge or consent.

"It's worth whatever someone is willing to pay for it."

"I really don't want to know what you were willing to pay for it." A chill slithered down her spine. "Why did you give it to him?"

"Why do you think?" As usual he looked calm and rather pleased with himself. Which under the circumstances could be adorable or infuriating, or both.

"To buy his approval of you having a relationship with me." No point in beating about the bush.

"I like the way you don't mince words." He squeezed her hands, which were either ice-cold, or boiling hot; she couldn't really tell anymore.

"But what if I don't want a relationship with you?" She tried to keep her voice steady while emotion threatened to close her throat. She wanted a relationship with him desperately. But not desperately enough to risk her independence, her self-esteem, her heart. "What if I feel a whole lot safer by myself?"

He frowned. "Dani, I won't ever force you to do anything you don't want to. I won't ever boss you around or treat you with anything less than the utmost respect. We can have it written into the marriage contract, if you like."

"Marriage?" Her voice emerged as a squeak. She'd seen this coming yet she still felt herself grow dizzy.

"I don't want you to be my girlfriend, or to reluctantly

accept a research grant from me. I love you. I want you to be my wife, my partner in life, my soul mate and the person I turn to every day to give and receive love and support." He inhaled a shaky breath. "Say you will, Dani. Please say you will."

She swallowed as conflicting emotions battled in her heart. "You just commanded me to say yes."

Confusion darkened his eyes. "I didn't mean it as a command. I was imploring you."

"Beseeching me." She giggled. Probably nerves. Quasar Al Mansur had just begged her to be his wife, and parted with millions to gain the privilege of asking her, and she had no idea what to say.

Of course her brain and body were screaming at her to agree.

Even though moments ago she'd been sure that she should calmly say no.

A weird shiver of excitement was rising from her toes, creeping up her limbs and torso and along her arms. Exciting possibilities unfolded before her—visions of a new life filled with love and hope and joy.

She *was* going to accept.

If this man loved her enough to do all this for her, it was worth the risk to take a leap of faith with him. "What was the question again? I'm not sure if you even asked me."

"Dani Hassan, will you be my wife?"

"Yes." She said it so fast it came out like a gasp. The sense of relief she felt afterward almost made her collapse in his arms. She'd made her decision and she knew in her heart that it was the right one.

He didn't say anything at all. His gaze softened and he inhaled a slow and steady breath. "Thank you. I promise I'll make you glad you married me." His wide, confident mouth broadened back into a smile, then she lost sight of it as he leaned in and kissed her with more passion than she'd ever dared to dream of.

Epilogue

Dani opened the front door, then stepped aside as the men burst into the house laughing and singing. Quasar led the way, followed by Dani's brothers, Khalid and Jalil, and Quasar's brothers, Elan and Salim. Her father brought up the rear in a rather dignified manner. "It's not easy to follow Omani wedding customs here in Boston," Quasar explained to her with a kiss. "We're really supposed to play drums, fire shots into the air and drive from my house to yours flashing our lights and honking horns the whole way, but I don't want us all to get arrested for disturbing the peace."

They'd decided to drive into Cambridge and cruise around MIT in a limo blasting the stereo instead.

"You should see the campus. It's awesome." Khalid's eyes shone with excitement.

"I have seen it." She grinned. "And if you don't want

to stay in one of the MIT dorms you could come live with us while you're studying there."

"Now, now." Her dad smiled sheepishly. "Khalid has to get in first. An application to MIT is no laughing matter."

"We all know Khalid is a genius." Quasar ruffled Khalid's hair. "And MIT will be lucky to get him."

White flowers ornamented almost every surface in the elegant brownstone. It was wonderful to see the place filled with life, even with noise and too many people trying to use the bathrooms at the same time. What a difference from the hushed and somber atmosphere at her first wedding, which her friends had warned her against and her cousins were forbidden to attend.

All the ladies had their hands hennaed the night before, another Omani tradition she'd skipped over last time. She expressed her admiration for the women, and Quasar came up behind her and gave her a kiss. "You look stunning."

It was the first time he'd seen her long white gown—even Omani brides usually wore white these days—with pearl beads sewn into swirling patterns on the skirt. Strapless and cut low in the back, it made her feel daring and sexy as well as beautiful.

She'd been so sure she'd never feel that way again, until she found Quasar reading the one book she wanted in her favorite bookstore. "It's so strange that I had to go back to Oman to find you."

"And that I had to go back to Oman to find you." He kissed her softly on the lips, then led her through the house and out into the decorated garden. The leafy canopy of old oak and maple trees filtered the bright afternoon sunshine. A white pavilion, decked with flowers, was set up for the imam to perform the brief marriage ceremony.

She couldn't believe how involved Quasar had been in planning the wedding. He really seemed to want to discuss every detail, even though he was in the middle of a deal big enough to make the front page of the *Financial Times*.

Salim, always one to take charge, moved through the gathered crowd, ushering them out into the garden. Celia and Sara organized the children around the pavilion with baskets of flower petals to toss at the moment the marriage became official.

"Where's my shawl? I don't think the imam wants to see my bare shoulders." Dani bit her lip and grinned mischievously.

"I put it under the pavilion so you'd have it when you needed it," answered Quasar. "Let me get it for you."

"What have you done to my brother?" asked Salim. "I don't remember him being thoughtful."

"He seems determined to prove to me that I'm making the right choice by marrying him."

"Determination is a core Al Mansur trait." Elan walked up, carrying little Hannah, whose eyes glittered with freshly dried tears. Fortunately her face also glowed with a dazzling smile. "It's particularly exasperating during the toddler years. But it's one of the things that makes us so loveable."

Quasar returned and draped the silky white chiffon carefully over her shoulders and hair. "See, you can be both traditional and modern at the same time."

"And American and Omani." She winked. They'd found a live band composed of Harvard students who swore they could play both traditional Omani music and classic rock. Just watching them try promised to be fun.

"The Al Mansur family is officially global," Sara chimed in.

"Speaking of the Al Mansur family, when do you plan to add to the lineage?" Celia moved next to Dani. "I think it's quite miraculous that Dani managed to get all the way to her wedding vows without getting pregnant."

"Or did she?" Sara raised a brow.

Dani laughed. "No plus signs on the pregnancy test for me. I've just started my job at the Harvard Art Museum Research Center and I'm hoping to travel to their ongoing excavation in Sardis next year. Besides, Quasar and I intend to enjoy each other for a while before we add to our family." She loved that he hadn't put any pressure on her at all to have children yet. They had plenty of time for that.

Quasar took her hand and they walked together along the stone path toward the pavilion where they'd be joined in marriage. Tears welled inside her, but this time they were tears of happiness.

* * * * *

*If you liked Dani and Quasar's story,
don't miss how his brothers met and fell in love with
their soul mates in these novels from USA TODAY
bestselling author Jennifer Lewis:*

*THE BOSS'S DEMAND
THE DESERT PRINCE*

All available now from Harlequin Desire!

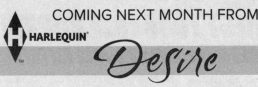
#2341 THE SECRET AFFAIR

The Westmorelands • by Brenda Jackson

Facing her family's disapproval, Jillian ended her affair with Dr. Aidan Westmoreland. But he knows their passion won't be denied—not for secrets or mistakes. And he'll follow her around the world to prove it...

#2342 PREGNANT BY THE TEXAN

Texas Cattleman's Club: After the Storm • by Sara Orwig

When Stella discovers she's pregnant from one passionate night with Aaron, she declines his dutiful marriage proposal. But the Dallas mogul lost one family already; he doesn't intend to lose this child—or Stella!

#2343 THE MISSING HEIR

Billionaires and Babies • by Barbara Dunlop

When tragedy struck, Amber took care of Cole's infant half brother. Yet a custody battle soon forces Cole to claim the child...and lie to the woman he can't seem to resist. Will he ever win Amber's trust?

#2344 CHRISTMAS IN THE BILLIONAIRE'S BED

The Kavanaghs of Silver Glen • by Janice Maynard

English beauty Emma broke Aidan Kavanagh's heart a decade ago. Now she's back—as a guest at his brother's Christmas wedding! Will the truth about her betrayal heal old wounds, or will she lose Aidan all over again?

#2345 SCANDALOUSLY EXPECTING HIS CHILD

The Billionaires of Black Castle • by Olivia Gates

Reclaiming his heritage means everything to Raiden Kuroshiro, until his passion for Scarlett Delacroix threatens all of his plans...and her life. Will he give up everything he thought he wanted to keep her and his baby?

#2346 HER UNFORGETTABLE ROYAL LOVER

Duchess Diaries • by Merline Lovelace

Undercover agent Dominic St. Sebastian learns he's technically a royal duke. But when the woman who discovered his heritage is attacked, leaving her with amnesia, it seems the only person the bewildered beauty remembers is him... _____

REQUEST YOUR FREE BOOKS!
2 FREE NOVELS PLUS 2 FREE GIFTS!

♦HARLEQUIN®

Desire

ALWAYS POWERFUL, PASSIONATE AND PROVOCATIVE

YES! Please send me 2 FREE Harlequin Desire® novels and my 2 FREE gifts (gifts are worth about $10). After receiving them, if I don't wish to receive any more books, I can return the shipping statement marked "cancel." If I don't cancel, I will receive 6 brand-new novels every month and be billed just $4.55 per book in the U.S. or $4.99 per book in Canada. That's a savings of at least 13% off the cover price! It's quite a bargain! Shipping and handling is just 50¢ per book in the U.S. and 75¢ per book in Canada.* I understand that accepting the 2 free books and gifts places me under no obligation to buy anything. I can always return a shipment and cancel at any time. Even if I never buy another book, the two free books and gifts are mine to keep forever.

225/326 HDN F4ZC

Name	(PLEASE PRINT)
Address	Apt. #
City	State/Prov.	Zip/Postal Code

Signature (if under 18, a parent or guardian must sign)

Mail to the **Harlequin® Reader Service:**
IN U.S.A.: P.O. Box 1867, Buffalo, NY 14240-1867
IN CANADA: P.O. Box 609, Fort Erie, Ontario L2A 5X3

Want to try two free books from another line?
Call 1-800-873-8635 or visit www.ReaderService.com.

* Terms and prices subject to change without notice. Prices do not include applicable taxes. Sales tax applicable in N.Y. Canadian residents will be charged applicable taxes. Offer not valid in Quebec. This offer is limited to one order per household. Not valid for current subscribers to Harlequin Desire books. All orders subject to credit approval. Credit or debit balances in a customer's account(s) may be offset by any other outstanding balance owed by or to the customer. Please allow 4 to 6 weeks for delivery. Offer available while quantities last.

HD13R

Here's a sneak peek of
THE SECRET AFFAIR
by New York Times *and* USA TODAY *bestselling author*
Brenda Jackson

Dr. Aidan Westmoreland entered his apartment and removed his lab coat. After running a hand down his face, he glanced at his watch, frustrated. He'd hoped he would have heard something by now. What if…

The ringing of his cell phone made him pause. It was the call he'd been waiting for. "Paige?"

"Yes, it's me."

"Is Jillian still going?" he asked, not wasting time with chitchat.

There was a slight pause on the other end, and in that short space of time knots formed in his stomach. "Yes, she's still going on the cruise, Aidan."

He released the breath he'd been holding as Paige continued, "Jill still has no idea I'm aware that the two of you had an affair."

Aidan hadn't known Paige knew the truth either, until she'd paid him a surprise visit last month. According to her, she'd figured things out the year Jillian had entered medical school. She'd become suspicious when he'd come home for his cousin Riley's wedding and she'd overheard him call Jillian Jilly in an intimate tone. Paige had been concerned this past year when she'd noticed

Jillian seemed troubled by something that she wouldn't share with Paige.

Paige had talked to Ivy, Jillian's best friend, who'd also been concerned about Jillian. Ivy had shared everything about the situation with Paige. Which had prompted Paige to fly to Charlotte and confront him. Until then, Aidan had been clueless as to the real reason behind his and Jillian's breakup.

When Paige had told him about the cruise she and Jillian had planned and she'd suggested an idea for getting Jillian on the cruise alone, he'd readily embraced it.

"I've done my part and the rest is up to you, Aidan. I hope you can convince Jill of the truth."

Moments later he ended the call and continued to the kitchen, where he grabbed a beer. Two weeks on the open seas with Jillian would be interesting. But he intended to make it more than just interesting. He aimed to make it productive.

A determined smile spread across his lips. By the time the cruise ended there would be no doubt in Jillian's mind that he was the only man for her.

*Find out how this secret affair began—and how
Aidan plans to claim his woman in
THE SECRET AFFAIR by New York Times and
USA TODAY bestselling author Brenda Jackson.*

*Available December 2014,
wherever Harlequin® Desire books and ebooks are sold!*

HDEXP1114